COVER SHEET — FAX

To: You
Subject: Let's Get Together
Date: Today
Pages: 1

Strictly Personal

Sweetheart,

Sorry this has gotten out of hand. We need to meet and talk this over before it goes any further. Meet me at the Century Country Club in Malibu at eight tonight, so we can try to work this out before either of us does something the other will regret....

—M.

Strictly Personal

From the Desk of:
Marsden Industries
California

Dear Reader,

Welcome to the world of technology, where the fax has replaced the phone—even for courting purposes. I have to admit, the most personal message *I've* ever received via fax was an exciting offer to order pastrami on rye from the new deli down the street. But hey, you can't judge everyone's life by mine! In Mary Anne Wilson's *Strictly Personal*, the hero's brother uses the fax to send a break-up note to the heroine's friend. But in a fortuitous case of mistaken identity, *he* thinks *she* is the woman scorned, and *she* thinks *he* is the cowardly brother. Why fortuitous? Because once they figure everything out, they... well, I'm not going to give the ending away, but suffice it to say you'll be glad they don't do *everything* electronically!

Hayley Gardner's back this month, too, with *The One-Week Baby*, her second FOR BETTER... FOR WORSE...FOR A WEEK! book. West Gallagher likes his bachelor ways, but his good times come to a screeching halt when a screeching *infant* lands on his doorstep. And as if that's not enough, the infant is quickly followed by Annie Robicheaux, a sexy lady lawyer who gets West's heart racing. All of a sudden, the seven days that had seemed interminable when he had to spend them caring for a baby were nowhere near long enough to prove to Annie how much he cared for her!

That's it this time around, but don't forget to come back next month for two more books all about unexpectedly meeting, dating—and marrying—Mr. Right.

Yours,

Leslie Wainger
Senior Editor and Editorial Coordinator

Please address questions and book requests to:
Silhouette Reader Service
U.S.: 3010 Walden Ave., P.O. Box 1325, Buffalo, NY 14269
Canadian: P.O. Box 609, Fort Erie, Ont. L2A 5X3

MARY ANNE WILSON

Strictly Personal

Published by Silhouette Books
America's Publisher of Contemporary Romance

If you purchased this book without a cover you should be aware that this book is stolen property. It was reported as "unsold and destroyed" to the publisher, and neither the author nor the publisher has received any payment for this "stripped book."

For Wendy Ferguson–
who deserves only the very best,
and we both know who that is!
Thanks for being a friend.

 SILHOUETTE BOOKS

ISBN 0-373-52048-4

STRICTLY PERSONAL

Copyright © 1997 by Mary Anne Wilson

All rights reserved. Except for use in any review, the reproduction or utilization of this work in whole or in part in any form by any electronic, mechanical or other means, now known or hereafter invented, including xerography, photocopying and recording, or in any information storage or retrieval system, is forbidden without the written permission of the editorial office, Silhouette Books, 300 East 42nd Street, New York, NY 10017 U.S.A.

All characters in this book have no existence outside the imagination of the author and have no relation whatsoever to anyone bearing the same name or names. They are not even distantly inspired by any individual known or unknown to the author, and all incidents are pure invention.

This edition published by arrangement with Harlequin Books S.A.

® and TM are trademarks of Harlequin Books S.A., used under license. Trademarks indicated with ® are registered in the United States Patent and Trademark Office, the Canadian Trade Marks Office and in other countries.

Printed in U.S.A.

Dear Reader,

The idea of a few words written on a single sheet of paper changing the lives of two people forever is a fascinating idea to me. Words changed my life years ago when I picked up my first romance, *Pride and Prejudice,* by Jane Austen, and met Elizabeth Bennet and Mr. Darcy, two people who, by all rights, should never have fallen in love. But when they did, I was hooked.

From when my first book, *Hot-Blooded,* was published by Intimate Moments ten years ago, through almost twenty-five subsequent books, I'm still hooked on the stories of two people finding each other in this world despite all the obstacles and all the logic that says they'll never make it.

Strictly Personal, the story of Genna and Nick, is as improbable as Elizabeth's and Mr. Darcy's story. Nick is a singular man who is going through life alone, satisfied with his choices. Genna is a sensible woman who knows that love is an illusion, a myth for others to believe in. But when these two people meet because of a fax that goes astray, their lives will never be the same.

If Elizabeth and Mr. Darcy could do it, Genna and Nick have a chance, and it was great fun bringing these two people together. I hope you enjoy reading *Strictly Personal* as much as I enjoyed writing it.

Mary Anne Wilson

Books by Mary Anne Wilson

Silhouette Yours Truly

Strictly Personal

Silhouette Intimate Moments

Hot-Blooded #230
Home Fires #267
Liar's Moon #292
Straight from the Heart #304
Dream Chasers #336
Brady's Law #350
Child of Mine #374
Nowhere To Run #410
Echoes of Roses #438
*Two for the Road #472
*Two Against the World #489
Jake's Touch #574

* Sister, Sister

Silhouette Shadows

False Family #45

Prologue

San Francisco, December 15

Belinda:
Merry Christmas. I've been trying to get you for ages, then remembered you might have had to work. Since your answering machine won't pick up, I thought I'd fax this to you so it will be waiting when you get back from your flight. I know things have been rough for you since the Robert fiasco, and I know I shouldn't say this, but that man was a jerk. You deserve better than someone who lies about being married, of all things.

Okay, no more about Robert. Now for the good news. I can get down there for Christmas, after all. Mom and Dad are heading for Florida to visit relatives, and I've managed to get another doctor to cover for me at the clinic, so I'll bring some good wine, my copy of *It's a Wonderful Life*, lots of gifts, and you get the turkey. I don't care if it's turkey sandwiches or frozen dinners.

Please tell me you have the holidays off for once and that you're not jetting to some far corner of the world.

Love, Genna

Los Angeles, December 16

Genna:
Just got in and found your fax. The answering machine broke down and since I'm heading out the door for another flight, I don't have time to get it fixed. So, fax it is. Fantastic that you'll be here for Christmas!

Yes, I've got three days off then. But one suggestion—bring champagne instead of wine. You're right. I do deserve better than the Roberts of this world, and I found him two weeks ago! I can't wait for you to meet him and see how good Santa has been to me this year. Let me know when you're flying in.

Ho, ho, ho, and Merry Christmas.

Love ya, Belinda

December 17

Belinda:
Whoa! You're moving too fast for me. I

thought you'd still be mourning Robert, and now you've got a mystery man. Slow down, and let's talk this over. You need a healing period, and getting into a relationship on the rebound is never a good idea. We'll talk this through as soon as I get there. My flight's on the 22nd, and I'll be there for dinner.

            Genna

December 18

Genna:
Forget all that shrink talk for once. I'm deliriously happy! When you meet Mars, you'll understand how just one look from a man can bring you to your knees. Someday I hope to see you fall hopelessly in love and forget you're a shrink.
 See you the 22nd.

            Belinda

December 19

Belinda:
This isn't professional advice, just advice from a friend who cares about you. Slow down, back up and rethink this whole thing. We can talk this all over while we trim the tree and wrap presents. Maybe we can retrieve some sanity

before everything explodes...again.

Genna.

P.S. Mars? As in the red planet or the Roman god of war?

December 20

Genna:
Bad news. You'll have to wait to "retrieve my sanity" until Christmas Eve. I just got the news that I have to fill in on a crew leaving LAX late on the 22nd, but I'll be here on the 24th. So, make yourself at home until I get back, and try to chill out.

I'll invite Mars over for Christmas dinner, and you can get to know him. Oh, by the way, that's a nickname, but the man fits a Roman god role to a tee. He's tall, blond, gorgeous, smart and fun. And get this...he's the son of the founder of Marsden Industries!!! Big bucks.

Try and talk me out of that with all your psychobabble. Love ya and I know you'll love Mars. Don't fuss too much about a present. I think I'm getting the present I want from Mars...with lots of sparkle. Can't wait for Christmas.

Belinda

December 21

Belinda:
I've just got two words for you. Remember Robert! This Mars is practically a stranger, and don't give me that ''love at first sight'' thing. There isn't such an animal. It's lust at first sight and nothing that's going to last.

I'll get in around five and hope to catch you before you leave. Please, I don't care how wonderful this man seems, or what you think he's going to do, or what you think he's going to give you. Don't do a thing you can't undo before I get there.

Love, Genna

Santa Monica, December 22, 5:15 p.m.

Genna Wade hurried up the stairs to Belinda's apartment, which occupied the entire second floor of an old house two blocks from Santa Monica Beach. She hoped against hope that she was in time to catch Belinda before she left for her flight. But when she let herself in, she knew she was too late. She could feel the emptiness all around her.

"Damn," she muttered as she dropped her bag and purse on the floor by the door, then flipped the light switch to her right.

The glow from an old-fashioned light fixture exposed what could have been a really attractive space, with hardwood floors, rough plaster walls and high ceilings. But that was all but lost under a layer of clutter and neglect that seemed to follow Belinda everywhere she went. Even the Christmas tree looked forlorn, sitting in front of the multipaned windows. It was maybe four feet tall, with a scattering of blue bulbs and skinny strands of gold tinsel.

Through an archway to the left that had a tiny sprig of mistletoe hanging from it, Genna could see the bedroom, another disaster area. And to the right was the other bedroom, loosely called an office, a remnant of Belinda's long gone desire to be a freelance travel agent. Now it was a dumping place for everything Belinda didn't know where to put.

Genna closed the door and had barely kicked off her low black heels when the phone rang. The sound was muffled, but unmistakable: an annoying cheeping sound that Genna remembered came from a phone that looked like a large set of red lips.

As she looked around, she saw the broken answering machine, sitting upside down on the floral couch by a pile of laundry, but no phone. Genna walked toward the sound, finally spotting the red lips half-hidden under a side table near the Christmas tree.

She grabbed for the receiver at the moment the ringing stopped and a series of electronic sounds came from the office. A fax. She quickly made her way across the room and into the room where the fax machine sat on a makeshift desk right by the computer. The receiving light was on, and paper started to come out of the back.

She almost turned away, but caught a glimpse of

a personal, handwritten message scrawled below the top banner of Marsden Industries. As she reached for the paper, she noticed her last fax to Belinda was still lying where it had come out at the bottom of the basket.

Genna scanned the strong black script on the stark white paper, and her hand began to shake.

From the first we agreed that when this wasn't fun anymore, it was over. I think the time has come to move on. Hey, Babe, it was great while it lasted and thanks for the laughs. Merry Christmas.

                                              Mars.

Genna's heart sank at the same time anger burned through her. "It's been fun?" she muttered, knowing that Belinda had, as usual, given her heart and soul to the wrong man. "Rotten, miserable bastard. Of all the low-down, cowardly things to do." Wine, old movies and presents weren't going to heal this hurt for Belinda.

Genna slowly crumpled the paper into a ball in her fist. If she and Belinda weren't closer than most sisters, if they hadn't been best friends since grade school, and if she didn't care, she would have walked out right then and never looked back. She didn't need the tears and hysteria that this breakup would produce from Belinda. But Genna couldn't just walk out and pretend that she'd never seen the message.

She looked down at the wad of paper in her hand. Belinda was an easy emotional target for men like Mars. Genna understood the syndrome. Her friend had been brought up in a series of foster homes and desperately wanted to belong. She wanted roots and was a classic case of emotional neediness.

The two women had met in grade school and had become friends instantly. But Genna, despite her degree in psychology, had never been able to stop Belinda from falling in love, over and over again. And experiencing disaster after disaster. Now she could add Mars to that list of disasters. How she hated him, even without ever having met the man. An irrational feeling, but very real, and it made her stomach churn.

She didn't care if Mars was rich, handsome and God's gift to women. To break off a relationship in this manner was beyond comprehension. Genna wanted to strike out, to not let him off the hook so easily.

Acting on human impulse rather than professional wisdom, she pushed aside some of the stacked newspapers on the makeshift desk. She smoothed out the crumpled-up piece of paper, found a return number at the top of the page, then switched on Belinda's computer. Genna quickly composed a letter to Mars, then printed it out.

Before rational thought could temper her actions, she placed her note into the fax machine, punched in the fax number for Mars, then hit Start.

"Coward," she muttered as she watched the paper feed through the machine. A part of her wished she had the man right here in front of her instead of on the other end of a fax line. But as angry as she was right now, it was probably better to have distance between her and this Mars person.

As the paper fell out of the fax into the basket, she knew that nothing was going to make this easier for Belinda. And despite the momentary pleasure she'd experienced just putting her anger down on paper, the reality of the situation was still there, hard and ungiving. She still had to deal with Belinda when she got home and found out that Mars had sent her a "Dear John" fax.

5:30 p.m. Los Angeles

Nicholas Marsden was finally leaving the offices of Marsden Industries, taking a much-needed break before making a late appointment. He had until nine o'clock to meet with Ron Weiss, the head negotiator for Xban, a production company Marsden Industries was trying to take over.

But he only got as far as the executive elevator

before Eileen, his assistant, called out behind him. "Boss? Wait up."

He turned as the tiny, gray-haired woman, dressed in her usual navy suit and sensible heels, came toward him looking uncharacteristically flustered.

"If it's Weiss wanting me to meet him before nine, tell him he'll just have to sit and wait for me. I need some food and time to think before we go at it again," Nicholas said.

"Wrong emergency," she said with her purse and jacket in one hand and a piece of paper in the other. She held the white sheet out in front of her, caught between her forefinger and thumb as if it was either very distasteful or reeked with some horrible odor.

"Okay, which emergency is this?"

"I was ready to leave but heard the fax machine running, so I went into the communications room to check on it. When I saw this message come through, I knew you had to see it before you left."

"No. I don't. It can wait. I'm leaving."

She continued to hold the paper between them. "So leave, but first take off your overcoat and take care of this."

The doors to the elevator slid open, and, refusing to be detained, Nick reached with his free hand to catch the doors and hold them open. "You take care of it."

"I can't," she said without any hesitation. "It's

about Mars." She paused, then quickly added, "And it's trouble."

Mars. Trouble. Slowly Nick let go of the doors and reached for the paper. He thought he had had his full dose of Mars and trouble earlier, when his younger brother had paid him an unexpected visit, but he'd been wrong...again. "What kind of trouble?" he asked as the elevator doors slid shut.

"Remember the stewardess? Well, she just faxed Mars, and she's not sending warm Christmas wishes."

Nick read the name and number stamp at the top of the page. "B. Hogan." Beneath it was a neatly typed letter addressed to Mars. But what he read wasn't neat at all. Mars had broken up with his latest girlfriend by fax and had sent that fax from the head office's communications room just before he left, less than half an hour ago.

> Mars: Are you so egotistical and self-centered that you think a fax is the way to break off a relationship? What happened to telling someone to her face that you lost interest and want to end the situation? What happened to decency? Just because you're a Marsden and are surrounded by money and power doesn't mean that you can get away with doing this.

There was no signature.

"That boy has sunk to a new low," Eileen muttered.

Nick couldn't argue with her statement. This wasn't only low, it was trouble with a capital *T*.

"You two, you look so much alike, but where you got moral fiber, he got spaghetti for a backbone," Eileen said.

"You're giving spaghetti a bad name," Nick teased.

Eileen frowned at Nick's six-foot-tall frame, his sandy hair and his clothes, a dark overcoat over a conservative, gray business suit. "I had no idea that's why he was using the fax machine. He just walked in, said he was sending a fax, then left. He never comes in here to do business. He probably doesn't even remember where his office is. I should have known he was up to no good."

Nick stared at the paper in his hand. *No good* was such an understatement. "Yeah, no good," he repeated.

"Just tell me where to reach him, Boss, and I'll get him back here in record time," Eileen said.

"I don't know where he is, or how to reach him," Nick said as he folded the paper in half. "He stopped by to tell me he was leaving for the holidays to go skiing. He said he had to work out something, then he asked for the company plane. When I told him it had to stay put here, he left. He never said where he was heading."

"Then what can we do? If you read between the lines, and if you understand how crazy Mars makes people, it's obvious she's out for blood...Marsden blood."

He shook his head, then motioned her toward the elevator. "Go on home, Eileen. I'll take care of this."

"Are you sure?"

"Absolutely." He pushed the Down button to summon the elevator for her, and the doors opened almost immediately. "Thank you for bringing this to my attention, Eileen. Have a wonderful night."

Eileen got into the elevator and turned back to Nick. "I guess it doesn't matter now, but your mother called and asked me to tell you to make sure that Mars got to the party on Christmas Eve an hour early so you can have family pictures taken."

"It doesn't matter at all," Nick said, especially since Mars had told Nick he wasn't going to make the party at all this year. He was going skiing instead.

As the elevator doors closed, Nick turned and walked back to his office. His work wasn't over. Mars was gone, God knew to what skiing resort he'd flown off to, leaving everyone else to take care of his problems.

As Nick stepped into his corner office on the fourteenth floor of the Marsden building, he tossed the paper onto the massive desk positioned to face the view out the floor-to-ceiling windows. "Enough is enough," he muttered.

He slipped out of his overcoat, laid it over the back of his leather chair, then sat behind the desk and uttered a scathing oath. Mars would be back sooner or later, but if the woman behind this letter was as angry as she sounded, she had to be headed off and pacified as quickly as possible.

The fury of a woman scorned. And this B. Hogan, dumped by fax, was definitely scorned. Telling his parents that Mars was a no-show for their annual party would be a walk in the park compared to the threat of this woman.

He turned his computer on, then quickly wrote a reply.

Sorry this has gotten so out of hand. We need to meet and talk this over before it goes any further.

Where could he meet this B. Hogan so they could talk, yet the probability of a scene wouldn't be too great? A busy, public place with lots of people around. The meeting would only be for a few minutes, then he would head over to meet Ron Weiss at the hotel.

Meet me at the Century Club in Malibu at eight tonight, so we can try to work this out before either of us does something the other will regret.

He printed it out, signed it, then went out to the com room and sent it off.

Any idea Nick had of taking a break before meeting with Weiss again was long gone. At eight he had to meet B. Hogan and hope he could find out just what sort of trouble she was going to make for the Marsdens. And stop her.

Genna heard the phone ring just as she finished packing the dishwasher. By the time she got into the living room, the fax machine clicked on. A single sheet of paper was waiting there, a piece of paper with the Marsden logo at the top.

She reached for it and read it quickly, frowning at the signature, an almost indecipherable scrawl, with only a capital *M* followed by an unrecognizable signature resembling a straight line. An egotistical man, a man who could break up by fax, then demand a meeting "...to work this out before either of us does something the other will regret." Genna knew he thought Belinda had sent the note back to him, and she didn't care.

She stared at the paper long and hard, then knew what she was going to do. She was going to meet the man, and despite the fact she wanted to rip into him and tell him just what she thought of him, she knew she couldn't. She was a trained psychologist, someone who was supposed to be able to understand people. If she met with Mars and figured him out, maybe she could talk him into breaking up in a way that would spare Belinda's feelings as much as possible.

Now she had to get to the Century Club at eight to meet a "tall, blond, gorgeous, smart, rich man." A real jerk.

Nick arrived at the Century Club in Malibu with five minutes to spare, his jacket and tie gone in favor of a leather windbreaker he kept in his car. He chose a small table near a massive bar that literally cut the former warehouse in two, separating the dining area from the main attraction, the dance club. He had a clear view of the entryway from where he sat, and kept watching for any woman who looked like Mars's type—tall, blond, leggy and flashy.

He fingered the cool condensation on his glass of Scotch and glanced around the club that was decidedly art deco. There was also a good dash of disco, down to and including a revolving glitter ball flashing colored lights around the huge space. Hard rock music from a live band bounced off the muraled walls.

As couples danced with abandonment on the hardwood dance floor, Nick saw a woman enter the club by herself. Tall, blond, pretty and almost trashy in a bright pink, glittering miniskirt and a top that looked like a liquid silver bra. He thought his wait was over until a man, a motorcycle type dressed in leather, came up behind her and kissed her on her neck before practically dragging her off to the dance floor.

Nick sipped more of his drink, the touch of a headache nudging behind his eyes as the music throbbed on and on. The thought of just leaving and letting the chips fall where they may was very inviting. But the chips wouldn't just fall at the feet of Mars. They would fall on top of the Marsden family.

He glanced at his wristwatch, then as he reached for his drink again his hand stilled on the cool glass as another woman came in. She seemed to be alone, too, but she couldn't be B. Hogan. She wasn't blond and was barely five and a half feet tall. In the glitter of the multicolored lights flickering around the room, he could see a mane of curly dark hair framing a delicately boned face. Underdressed in contrast to the other women in the club, she was wearing plain dark slacks, a light-colored silky-looking blouse with full sleeves and a simple V-neckline. Classy.

Holding a small purse to her middle, she glanced around the room, then finally started across in the direction of the bar. Even the way she moved demanded his attention, a subtle sexiness in the sway of her hips and the way she lowered her eyes as she made her way to one of the few empty stools at the bar. By the time the stranger sat down, B. Hogan was slipping farther from his mind.

He'd never been one to pick up women in bars, to go through old lines like "What's your sign?" or "Don't we know each other?" He'd never sat in bars looking for women, for that matter. Even though women came and went, slipping in and out of his life, one of his rules was that life was too short to be like Mars. He'd never had the inclination to do what Mars did so well. He never had and never would. But as he watched this woman brush at her hair with one slender hand, then lean forward to talk to the bartender, he realized that there were exceptions to every rule.

Since he had to wait for Mars's girlfriend to show up, and he didn't have to be at the hotel until nine, he had a little bit of time to kill. And he knew there was a better way of killing the time than just sitting here nursing a drink.

Genna hated places like the Century Club. Smoke hung in the air. Loud music assaulted her ears, and she knew that any meaningful conversation with Mars would be impossible. But, then again, so would a knock-down-drag-out fight.

Mars had picked his place for this confrontation. And she found herself disliking him even more. He was a man in control of everything, it seemed. Including Belinda. Genna made her way across the crowded room to one of the very few empty stools at the impressive, mirror-backed bar. As she slid onto the high seat, she had barely laid her purse on the polished top before the bartender was there.

She looked up at the guy who was barely old enough to drink, let alone serve alcohol. Dark shorts and a bright fuchsia tank top with the club's logo on it showed off a weight lifter's build and an incredibly dark tan, even for California. The man looked for all the world as if he belonged stripping on ladies' night, even when he smiled brilliantly at her.

"What would you like, sweetheart?" he asked.

She knew the stock answer was probably "You," but there wasn't much appeal there. Not when she felt tied in knots with the anticipation, or maybe a better word would be *dread* of her upcoming meeting with Mars.

"Mineral water with a twist of lemon," she said, raising her voice a bit to be heard over the cacophony of noise.

The smile grew brighter as he said, "Great choice," gave her a thumbs-up sign with a wink, then moved away to get her drink.

She looked at the smoky mirrors on the wall behind the bar and scanned the room's reflection. In the crush of partyers, she saw more than a few tall, blond and gorgeous men. But none of them seemed to be looking as if they were trying to find a particular woman.

She was intent on watching for Mars when she was startled by someone talking from right beside her. "Hey, Baby, you can stop looking right now. You've found the guy you came here to meet."

2

Genna turned to her right, bracing herself to face down Mars, but instead there was a grinning drunk on the next stool, leering at her. He was certainly no blond god. He was short and dark and looked as if he might be fifty or more. And he reeked of alcohol.

He eyed her up and down suggestively, then nodded. "It's true. You've been waiting for me all your life, sweetcakes. Admit it."

Like I've been waiting for the black plague all my life, she thought, but settled for saying, "I'm sorry. I thought you were my husband."

He uttered a single word that said it all, then shook his head. "Later, sweetcakes." Then he grabbed his drink and slipped off the stool. He had to pause to get his balance before he headed off to prowl the rest of the room.

"Here you go, honey." Genna looked away from the drunk to the bartender who slipped a frosty glass in front of her. "That'll be two-fifty."

She took a five-dollar bill out of her purse and laid it on the bar. "Thanks," she said.

The bartender picked up the money and slipped it into his pocket without a mention of bringing her change. "Thank you. I'm Maurice, and you just call if you need my services again," he said with another wink. Then he walked off with her money.

Another lesson, she thought as she took a sip of the very expensive water, then put her glass back down and glanced into the mirrors again. As she looked toward the side of the room to a cluster of small cocktail tables, she felt her breath catch. She spotted a man sitting alone and looking around the room. He fit Belinda's description to a tee.

He appeared tall, probably six foot at least if he was standing, and his dark blond hair was combed straight back from a sharp, angular face. If he was Mars, *hunk* was hardly an adequate word. In a well-worn leather jacket over an open-necked pale shirt, he was devastatingly male...even across the crowded room and reflected in smoky mirrors.

As he slowly looked away from the drink in his hand and glanced toward the bar, Genna felt his gaze suddenly lock with hers in the mirror. The impact of the connection startled her so much she quickly looked away.

Boy, she hoped this guy wasn't Mars. Her anger had carried her this far, but she couldn't deal with a man who made her heart race and her mouth go dry instead of making her raging mad. She quickly took another sip of the water, wishing she'd ordered something alcoholic, after all. She could have used the fortification, especially if she was going to have to get up, go to that man and confront him.

She put down the glass and closed her eyes as she took a couple of deep breaths to regain her composure, but before she looked back at him, someone spoke to her.

"Excuse me?" a deep, male voice said close to her right ear.

She jumped and her eyes flew open. She expected to see the drunk again, persistent and obnoxious, but she was very wrong. At the same moment she inhaled a clean, masculine fragrance, she saw the man she'd seen in the mirrors...right behind her, bending close enough to be heard. Now she could tell his eyes were a deep, almost navy, blue, and the sense of sexiness she'd felt at a distance was magnified a hundredfold this close.

Mars? Everything fit, except her own reaction to his slow smile and seductively endearing expression. If this man was Mars, she could see exactly why Belinda had fallen so hard for him. Still, a part of her hated him for being able to smile like that when he was well on his way to destroying her best friend.

But why jump to conclusions? What if he wasn't Mars? What if he was a perfect stranger standing there smiling at her and had nothing to do with the Marsden family at all?

He never looked away from her as he leaned even closer and spoke in her ear, the heat of his breath brushing her skin and sending shock waves through her. "Is this seat taken?" he asked, motioning to the stool vacated by the drunk earlier.

Genna shook her head as she tried to ease her grip on the cool glass in her hands. "No," she managed to say.

"Can I buy you another drink?" he asked.

She forced herself to look right at him, unnerved that his knees were only inches from hers as he settled on the stool next to her. If he was Mars, she needed this contact before he figured out who she was. And alcohol just might help a bit. "Sure. A...a gin gimlet."

He motioned to the bartender, placed the order, adding a Scotch for himself, then looked back at her. "I don't usually do this," he murmured.

She couldn't take her eyes off him. "Excuse me?"

"I hardly ever come to bars, and I can't remember the last time I offered to buy a stranger a drink."

It was a line, pure and simple. She wondered how he'd picked up Belinda, what he'd said to her, if he smiled at her like this and pretended that he'd never done it before. "I can't remember the last time I let a man I didn't know buy me a drink," she said in response.

"Then I should change that right now. Let me introduce myself formally, then you'll know me," he said.

But before he could say anything else, the bartender returned with their drinks. Genna watched as he paid for them with a large bill, and the change was made by the bartender immediately. The stranger nudged a five-dollar bill toward the bartender, then turned to Genna as he lifted his drink. With a crooked smile he said, "I'm Nicholas Marsden."

Genna knew that disappointment was a stupid reaction to his effectively blowing away any doubts she'd harbored about his identity. While he took a sip of his Scotch, she tried to get her bearings.

Suddenly he looked at her with a half smile. "Now, you're suppose to tell me your name."

"Genna Wade," she said after a long silence. She waited for him to recognize her, but he looked as if he'd never heard of her before. Either Belinda hadn't mentioned her to him, or he hadn't listened. "Genna?" he asked. "A nickname?"

"No, just Genna," she said. Then, holding her drink between her palms, she asked, "What do they call you—Nick, Nicky, Nicholas...or maybe Mars?"

He frowned slightly at that. "I've been called all

of those things in my life, but I'd prefer you called me just Nick."

How about Mr. Wrong? she thought with bitterness resting on her tongue. She picked up her drink, unsettled to see that her hand wasn't quite steady, and quickly took a sip. Coolness mixed with subtle warmth as the liquid slid down her throat.

Every word she'd rehearsed in the rental car on the way over here was mysteriously gone. None of them fit. And her mind refused to focus. Nervous, she spoke to fill the silent spaces around them until she could figure out exactly what to do. "You said you hardly ever come here?"

"Hardly ever," he echoed. That smile was back again, just as affecting and just as treacherous for her. "Believe me, I really didn't come to hit on someone."

She felt heat brush her cheeks, but kept her gaze up. "Then why *did* you come?"

"I had an appointment, but..." He shrugged as if it was of little importance to him. "I'm not at all sure she's going to show up."

"She?"

"It's something that needs to be taken care of, but it's nothing personal."

Her stomach tightened. "Then what is it, if it's—"

He cut her off with a shake of his head. "It's not

important, that's what it is. Actually, it's something I'd like to forget about if I could.''

Genna took the last sip of her drink and was surprised that her mind was getting clearer. Not important? Something he wanted to forget about? He was here to meet and talk to Belinda about their relationship, yet he was hitting on her...and hitting hard.

He might be painfully sexy and sending her hormones into overdrive, but he was still a cold-blooded bastard. A man who thought he could get away with anything with any woman he wanted, just by smiling and turning on the charm. He obviously liked the chase and the challenge, but nothing affected his heart if he could treat Belinda so offhandedly and coldly.

All she could think of was what she could do to wipe that smile off his face. Telling him off, here and now, suddenly seemed too trite, too pat. Besides, he would just walk away unscathed when it was over.

"Another drink?" he asked, motioning to her empty glass.

She nodded. "Yes, thanks." She could use it.

As Nick motioned to the bartender, Genna was faced with a realization that shocked her, making her very thankful for how quickly the bartender gave her a fresh gin gimlet. She took a drink as she tried to absorb what she was thinking now.

Revenge. That's what she wanted. But that didn't make sense. She'd come here to figure him out, to try and soften the blow for Belinda; yet with every second that passed, she knew that she wanted revenge for Belinda, and maybe a bit of revenge for herself. Something to make up for the way he could attract her so easily.

Revenge was a foreign concept to her and went against every professional instinct in her. But that didn't stop the feeling from being there. As he kept talking about the music or something very neutral, she knew that whether it was sensible or not, revenge was what she was going to get.

"So, what do you think?" he asked her.

"Excuse me?"

"I was just wondering what you thought of this music," he said with a crooked smile.

"It's numbing," she muttered as she reached for her drink again. And she wondered how much he would smile if he was the one on the receiving end of a brush-off, if a woman he was interested in cut him off rudely and cruelly? She knew men his type, men who couldn't take anything that affected their image or self-esteem. Anything that affected their delusion that they could do anything they wanted to do.

The smile only deepened on his face and intensified her reaction to him. "I thought perhaps it was just me, that I was getting too old to appreciate this kind of music."

"Age has nothing to do with it." The alcohol was taking the edges off, but nothing could stop the effect that smile was having on her. "It's pretty awful."

"My thoughts exactly," he said.

Her thought was far from the music. She realized that if she was going to do anything to get to this man, she had until Christmas Eve to do it. Then Belinda would be home.

Nick leaned closer to her. Genna had to fight the urge to move away, to keep some buffer of safety between them and fight inhaling a certain maleness that seemed to cling to him. The smile shifted to slow and sensual, rocking Genna with its impact. "It makes you long for a good old ballad or two, doesn't it?"

Genna knew right then exactly what she was going to do, and before she could rethink her actions, she reached for her purse. "Excuse me. I...I'll be right back," she murmured, and slipped off the stool. "I need to freshen up."

Quickly she headed toward a flashing arrow near the bar that pointed to the back restaurant area. Once she was on the back side of the bar, out of sight from Nick, she stopped and motioned to another bartender, a longhaired bodybuilder type.

"Yes, luv?" he asked with a wide smile and a heavy Australian accent. "What can I do you for?"

"A favor?"

He grinned at her. "Anything, luv."

"There's a blond man, tall, dark blue eyes, sitting on the other side of the bar nursing a Scotch. His name is Mr. Marsden. Would you take a message to him?"

He leaned on the bar with both hands and got close to her. "And what would that message be?"

"Could you tell him there was a phone call from Belinda Hogan. She won't be able to make their appointment. Everything's over, and she's getting on with her life."

"Anything else?"

Genna took a five-dollar bill out of her purse and held it out to him. "Just make sure he doesn't know that I'm the one who gave you the message."

He looked down at the money and took it from her, then tucked it into his pocket. "Games?" he murmured suggestively.

"Something like that."

"Okay, on with the games." He winked at her, then headed off around the end of the bar.

"On with the games," Genna echoed, the idea distasteful to her, but not as distasteful as what Belinda would walk into when she got back. She turned and crossed to the rest rooms.

In the pink marble space, she stood by the sinks

that lined one wall and turned on the cold water. Cupping the water in her hands, she splashed her face. As she blotted at the moisture with a paper towel, she looked at her reflection in the mirror.

She hadn't changed on the outside at all. She was still Dr. Genna Wade. Yet she knew that something in her had snapped, the moment she'd come face-to-face with Mars or Nick or whatever he wanted to call himself.

She'd come here to tell the man off, maybe even to make a scene, scream a bit, embarrass him...but mostly to help Belinda. She hadn't intended to start her own game of seduction and retribution. But that's exactly what she was preparing herself to do.

Nick listened to the bartender, unable to believe that his life had just simplified this dramatically. "When did she call?"

"A few minutes ago. I didn't see you around here, or I would have brought you the phone."

Relief filtered into Nick. The woman was gone. She wasn't a threat. She'd come to her senses and let go gracefully. He smiled as he took a bill out of his wallet and handed it to the bartender. "Thank you very much for the message."

As he pushed the money into his pocket, the bartender grinned at him. "It looks like it's good news for you."

"Very good."

"Way to go, man," he said with a thumbs-up sign. Then he left.

Nick barely had time to absorb the turn of events when he felt the vibration of his ringing cell phone in his jacket pocket. He pulled it out and snapped it open. He had to plug one ear with his finger to hear anything on the line. "Yes?"

He could barely make out Eileen on the line. "Just got a forwarded call," she said.

He hunched toward the bar, trying to make out what she was saying. "From Mars?"

"No. No word on that front. It's from Mr. Weiss."

The relief of B. Hogan's canceled meeting was dissolving very quickly. "What does he want now?"

"He wanted to let you know he's been called out of town until Christmas Eve. He says it's a family emergency."

Weiss was playing games, and Nick knew it. A part of him admired the man's guts to let the merger simmer for a couple of days, but part of him was angry at being manipulated. "Is that it?"

"He said to tell you he'd see you at the party on Christmas Eve."

"Great," he muttered. "You get him on the phone and tell him that won't fly. I don't care where his is, but tell him I won't wait until the party. Either he gives me a meeting tonight or tomorrow morning, or forget the whole thing." Two people could play this game. "If he won't do it, tell him we'll move on."

"But, he told me—"

"I don't care what he said," he said evenly, but firmly. "Don't let him put you off."

"Okay. What did you do about your brother's mess?"

"I came to meet with the woman to see if I could talk reason to her and maybe ease out of this mess."

"Use the famous Marsden persuasive powers on her?"

"Try to talk sense to her, Eileen."

"If you can handle Weiss, I think you can handle a stewardess."

"The stewardess problem is well under control."

"I won't even ask how you did it. I don't want to know the gory details. But it's good news, that's for sure."

Nick glanced at the mirrors and caught a glimpse of Genna coming around the end of the bar. As he turned to look at her making her way through the crush of people, he said, "Yes, actually, very good news. Just contact Weiss and tell him it's now or never."

"Yes, sir."

He flipped the phone shut, and as he slipped it back into his pocket, he realized that a woman he'd never met, and never would meet now, had done him a real favor tonight. Because of the woman faxing him, he was here. And now, because of Weiss trying to play mind games, he had some extra time to kill. Usually any downtime was hard on him, leaving him at wit's end with the need to get on with things, but this time it was different.

As he followed Genna's movements, he realized that it had been a long time since he'd considered having more to do with a woman than the obvious. A very long time. And right now he felt suspiciously like a teenager in the throes of a hormone rampage. He couldn't remember feeling like this since college.

Actually, it was more than that. He knew lusting after an attractive woman was one thing, but there'd never been a woman who had demanded his attention this intensely and this immediately. A meeting that was going to be short and interesting had just changed into a lot more.

When she gave him a slight smile as she got back onto the stool, he felt further encouraged. She turned to glance around at the crowded room. "This place is certainly very popular," she said, raising her voice to be heard over the din of others talking, laughing, and the overlay of loud music.

"Do you like to dance?" he asked.

She darted a veiled look from under ridiculously long lashes as the music reached a crescendo of drums and electric guitars while the dancers gyrated wildly. "I've never had the knack for moving to songs like this. The noise could kill plants or at least stunt their growth.''

He smiled at her and felt the tension of his day begin to fall away. But when she smiled back at him, another, more subtle tension started to grow. ''Definitely plant killers,'' he said, then offered impulsively, ''How about getting out of here and going someplace where we can hear each other talk?''

She shrugged, a fluttery motion of her slender shoulders under the clinging silk of her blouse. ''I don't know.''

He could feel the hesitation in her, and he found himself coaxing her. A man who closed multimillion-dollar deals by bluffing, by threatening to walk without looking back, and here he was coaxing this woman to get her to come with him. ''I know this isn't the safe thing to do—to go off with a stranger. But we can go to a very public place and get to know each other...as long as the music is soft and easy.''

''You—you have your friend coming.''

He brushed that aside easily. ''But I don't.''

She raised one fine eyebrow. ''I thought you said—''

''She canceled.''

The music stopped for a moment right when she said, ''That's too bad.''

''Actually, it's just fine with me,'' he said truthfully. ''I wasn't looking forward to it.''

"And that's that?" she asked, her eyes narrowed on him.

"I hope so."

"That's that," she repeated as she lifted her drink again.

She drank the last of her gimlet, and he found himself actually getting nervous. He wanted her to come with him to another place, where he could look at her and talk to her and get to know her. And he knew that he was violating one basic truth in negotiating for anything in this life.

Never get emotionally involved in the outcome of any negotiations. Once you did, you had no power. You were dealing from a place of weakness. As he looked at Genna—the sweep of her throat, the way delicate strands of dark hair brushed her milky skin at her temples—he knew that his emotional involvement was a given here.

And that admission made him even more nervous.

3

Nick knew that Genna had all the power right then, and that was only underscored when her dark eyes swept back to him, and the smile was there again. Another thought hit him and hit him hard. He hadn't even stopped to think about why she was here...if it was to meet a man who was waiting to see this very expression from her. Or a man who wanted nothing more than to touch her, to hold her, or to—

Nick cut that thought off and tried to regroup. "I never asked why you're here," he said.

"I was just getting out for a while."

"Alone?"

"Alone."

He almost breathed a sigh of relief and forged right on. "Will you come someplace else where the music is slow and easy and the food's great?"

Her lashes swept lower for a moment, then he was the victim of the full impact of her gaze. He could feel himself falling even deeper, weaker, and his body was treacherously close to emphasizing that very point as she asked in a husky voice, "Where do you have in mind?"

Bed. The single word shot through him, and he fought to say something that would distract his mind from wandering into territory that only made him more uneasy. "The Gentry. A little place up the coast. Nice, quiet, good food, a view and great music."

"You know, we barely met, and I'm not sure—"

"That I'm not a serial killer or some sort of psycho?"

One finely arched eyebrow lifted in his direction, but there was no accompanying smile. "Well, are you?" she asked with real seriousness.

He tried to play it off. "Serial killer? No."

"Psycho?"

"Not recently."

"Then what are you?"

"The worst thing I've been accused of is being a workaholic."

"That doesn't add up," she said.

"What's that?"

"A workaholic in a place like this, then wanting to go someplace quiet to talk. Shouldn't you be asking for a phone or checking your daily planner or making plans for your next big meeting?"

"The big meeting's been canceled for now."

"The woman who didn't show?"

"No, that's another meeting altogether. I was talking about a business meeting I had in—" he checked his watch "—half an hour. But he just canceled."

"Then you're at loose ends until more work shows up?"

"You've got it. And I'd like to just sit and talk for a while. But not here. So, how about it?"

She fingered her glass on the bar, and he felt his breath closing off in his lungs. Until she finally nodded. "Okay, someplace quiet."

He exhaled in a rush, thankful the action was masked by the band as they started another set. He leaned closer to Genna. "Let's go out of here before our hearing's impaired permanently." For a moment he seemed surrounded by her scent, light and flowery, and the impulse was there to move even closer, to find out just how her softly parted lips tasted.

For one disconcerting moment, he thought she'd read his mind, as she seemed to move closer to him. Then he realized that she was actually slipping off the stool to stand to face him. "Let's," she said with a nod as she turned from him to start across the crowded room.

He followed after her, making his way through the crowd of customers, staying a few steps behind her. He'd thought that nothing could rival the impact of her eyes on him, but from this angle, she was still affecting him on a basic level that defied reason. She walked quickly, her slacks softly hugging her hips and legs, and she held her head up just a bit. Seductive and sexy.

The sight of her made him want to slip his arm around her slender shoulders and feel her against his side. To see how she felt against him, how she tasted. But he kept behind her as they went up the few steps to the marble entryway. When an attendant opened the doors, Nick followed Genna out into the night.

The cool December air, touched by the pungency of the nearby beach, was scented with the fragrance of pine Christmas trees laced with multicolored twinkle lights that framed the entrance. Genna stopped on the sidewalk, and Nick was right by her side, looking down into her face, where the multicolored lights played across her delicate features.

Her eyes were any color, dark and fathomless. Shadows created faint hollows at her cheek and throat, and her full bottom lip seemed incredibly sensuous.

"Car, sir?" someone asked.

Nick jerked around as if he'd been burned by the intrusion.

A towheaded kid in a bright red jacket and tight black pants was smiling at them. Nick handed him his valet slip and murmured, "Black Porsche."

"Yes, sir," the kid said brightly, then jogged off in the direction of the parking area.

Nick turned back to Genna, meeting her partially shadowed gaze. Had he ever simply looked at a woman he'd never touched and been bombarded with images of what it must be to make love with her? He knew the answer to that before the question fully formed. He'd never been as attracted to a woman as he was to Genna, and never more interested in knowing everything about her.

"How about your car?" he asked, his mundane words belying the way he could feel his heart speed up and his body start to tighten from her closeness.

"I can leave it here, then come back to get it."

"Great," he said as he heard the roar of the Porsche engine coming toward them.

She turned as the black car pulled up to the curb with a screech of tires, then the kid jumped out. "Great wheels, man," he said as he went around and opened the passenger door for Genna. "Totally radical. Awesome pipes."

"Thanks," Nick said, exchanging the boy's tip for the key.

While Genna slipped into the car, Nick went around to get behind the wheel. He settled on the low leather seat, and as he closed the door he noticed that although Genna had only been in the car for mere seconds, her scent was already beginning to touch the air.

He looked over at her as she reached out and touched the dash lightly with the tips of her fingers.

The action brought the idea to him that he'd love to have her touch him like that. Light, feathery, exploring.

His body tightened again, and he admitted to himself that this was worse than he thought. He'd been in the corporate tower too damned long while Mars had had all the fun. Or maybe he'd just never met anyone like Genna before. Or a combination of both. He looked at the road as she drew her hand back to her lap.

"Great wheels, man," she said out of the shadows, mimicking the kid's voice perfectly, down to and including the touch of "valley" twang in the words. "Totally radical. Awesome pipes."

He laughed, really laughed, for the first time in what felt like a very long time. "That's terrific. Do you do Jimmy Cagney impersonations, too?"

"No, just people I hear around me," she said as she sat back in the leather seat. When he glanced at her, she cast him a sweeping glance. "I'd love to try and do you."

"Excuse me?" he said, his hand tightening on the gearshift.

"Your voice," she said evenly.

Sure, of course that's what she meant. He put the car into gear and drove off toward the Coast Highway. "Go ahead, do me," he said as he pressed the gas and felt the car instantly respond with a surge of power.

"I would, but I hardly know you," she said.

"Then let's remedy that. Ask me anything you want to know about me," he said as he got onto the highway and headed north. "Then you'll have material for this impersonation."

He could sense her shift in the seat, then he knew she was looking at him. He didn't have to turn to be aware of her eyes on him or how easily it would be to just reach out and touch her. "How about your appointment?"

"What about it?" he asked, his eyes on the highway ahead.

"The first one was with a woman, wasn't it?"

"Yes."

"Business or personal? You never actually said which."

He hesitated, not wanting to think about Mars and his troubles right then. Not when he was getting the distinct feeling of being in another world with this woman in his car. "Neither."

"What does that mean?"

He shrugged. "It means that I was meeting someone to end something and make sure the ending was clean and trouble free."

"Oh, an old girlfriend you were dumping," she said through the shadows in a slightly tight voice.

Her words cut too close to the truth about Mars to suit him. "Can I tell you a secret about me?"

She was silent for a moment, and he chanced a

look at her. She wasn't watching him, but facing straight ahead, her eyes on the night outside. "Yes, I think I'd like that," she finally said in a soft voice.

He took a breath, catching at her scent in the air again. "I'm not good at games."

"Games?" she echoed.

"Maybe that's the wrong word. I don't like to hedge and play around. I'm pretty direct. It works in business, and I think it works on a personal level."

"Oh, I understand. You tell it like it is?"

He winced at the old saying. "I prefer to think that I'm up-front about everything."

"Oh, and you never bluff or hedge the truth?"

Another direct strike. "Okay, I do bluff when I need to, but I only bluff when I'm prepared to go ahead with the bluff if my hand's called."

"So you lie?"

"No, I don't lie."

"Okay, then what did you want me to know about you?"

"I told you I don't go to bars to pick up women."

"So that means you really do go to bars to pick up women?"

He smiled at that. "No, I don't. I haven't been in a bar, except on business, for so long I can't remember when I was in one just for pleasure."

"You're telling me that you never have fun?"

He shrugged, wondering if he'd ever had

fun...until now? Certainly he wasn't on a par with Mars when it came to playing. "Not very often."

"But my guess is you don't live the life of a monk."

He chuckled at her comment. "Not even close."

"Are you trying to tell me you're married?" she asked directly, which took him aback for a moment.

"No, I'm not married."

"I thought this might be your way of breaking that bit of news to anyone you met at a bar."

He couldn't hear joking in her tone of voice, but she had to be kidding. "If I were married, I wouldn't have been in a bar in the first place, and in the second place, I wouldn't be here with you now."

"A virtuous man?" she muttered.

He didn't understand where this was coming from. "Far from it. I'm just saying that married is married."

"And that's a commitment."

"Absolutely."

"But until you get married, you can do what you want to do."

"I'm free to do whatever I like," he said, the lack of humor in their conversation stunning. The atmosphere in the car felt tense, and he was at a loss to understand why. "How about you?"

"What about me?"

"Married?"

"No," she answered honestly.

"Engaged then?" he questioned.

"No, are you?"

Nick shook his head. "No." He downshifted as they neared the beach area. "I hope this is all helping."

"Helping?"

"To get past that 'stranger' thing."

"Well, I think I'm closer to understanding you," she said, as if unsure she was really grateful to gain this personal information about him.

Did the woman ever say anything that he expected...that didn't take him off guard? "You think you understand me? I'm not sure I like that."

"I guess everyone thinks they're hard to understand. But that's not so. Everyone's pretty basic, their characters and motives." She took a soft breath, and when he felt her flash him a look, he determinedly kept his eyes on the road. "Maybe you want new ground rules?"

He did glance at her then and found her looking right at him, her eyes lost in shadows. But that didn't lessen the impact. "Such as?" he murmured.

"A rule about how honest we want to be with each other."

"Degrees of honesty? Now there's a business concept. I'm not sure I like it on a personal level," he muttered as he looked away from her.

"Okay, how about total honesty, but limits on what can be asked?"

He had the distinct feeling of being in some big business negotiation with a great amount on the line, but this was just a woman he'd met. Someone he wanted to know better. Certainly not crucial. But he couldn't shake the feeling that it could be. "You can ask me anything you want, and I can ask you anything I want. But neither one of us can ask about the other's past mistakes. Is that acceptable?"

"So now the woman who canceled was a mistake?"

"Monumental," he said.

He didn't know what he'd expected, but it wasn't that Genna would say, "That's pretty awful if a woman finds out that she's a mistake to someone she must have cared for."

He slanted her a glance and was struck by how tight her expression seemed in the low glow from the dash lights. "I didn't say I cared for her. I never even—"

"No, forget it. Past mistakes. Gone, over, done." She brushed her hands off as if she could banish the past with that action. "How's that?"

He looked back at the highway in front of them. "Fine by me." He flexed his fingers, which had tightened on the steering wheel. "How about starting this again?"

She shifted in the seat, stirring the air around him. "Okay."

"Are you from around here?" he asked.

"No. I'm from San Francisco, and just visiting for the holidays."

"Do you get down here often?"

"Every few months." He heard her sigh, before she said softly, "Although this time it's been way too long."

"Where are you staying?"

She hesitated, he could almost feel it in the air, then she said, "I don't know you well enough to tell you that just yet."

His hands tightened on the steering wheel again. "Okay, let's leave that alone for a while. What do you do for a living?"

"I'm a psychologist."

A doctor? She wasn't like any doctor he'd ever been around before. "Oh, that's why you thought you understood me. What am I, a classical version of some personality type?"

"In a way," she murmured.

"Enlighten me, then."

"You admitted you're a workaholic. That means you're a person who compartmentalizes his life. Never the twain shall meet, sort of thing. You don't get deeply involved in relationships because that takes commitment, and your commitment is to your work. I'd say relationships get in the way of that commitment, so you get what you want out of a relationship, then move on. And you will move on, every time you get too close to anyone.

"You'd rather be negotiating a business contract than dancing. You'd like to have the cell phone surgically implanted in your ear. You probably think you're reasonable, responsible and reliable, but others see you as single-minded, hardheaded, hard-hitting and shut off. I'd say a woman doesn't stand a chance of not getting dumped by you sooner or later."

He stared straight ahead, the thoughts she shot at him hitting their mark with frightening accuracy. "Whew, how about my bad traits?" he said, a bit tightly.

"Oh, I'm sorry. I got rather carried away," she admitted, but he had the oddest feeling that she wasn't sorry at all.

"Just as long as you don't bill me for that." He flexed his fingers. Of all the women in that bar, the only one he'd been attracted to was a hard-as-nails psychologist. "And don't set me up with another appointment for analysis."

She laughed, a low, soft sound. "No charge. And no follow-up appointment."

"Do you have your own practice?"

"Yes," she said.

"I always thought it took years and years before you could have your own practice."

"It takes long enough."

He looked at her again. "You don't look old enough to be a doctor."

"I'm twenty-nine. How old are you?"

"Thirty-five."

"What do you do?"

"Work," he muttered.

"I knew that, just by the fact a workaholic has to have work to be a workaholic. It follows."

"Okay, I manage the family business."

"Oh, a workaholic in the mob?"

He couldn't help laughing at that. He sure had his work cut out for him with this beauty. "No, the Marsden family business, Marsden Industries. I took over from my father five years ago."

"Oh, one of *those* Marsdens? As in big business, lots and lots of businesses? Merging with and taking over businesses right and left?"

"An informed psychologist," he murmured.

"I just read the business sections sometimes," she said, then shifted directions. "So one of the Marsdens was in the bar taking care of a little personal business, or did it leak over into family business?"

Dammit, she could hit bull's-eyes blindfolded with her questions. "Both. It had to be taken care of as quickly as possible and as quietly as possible."

"You really make it sound more and more like a mob hit."

He downshifted as he neared the area of the restaurant, and wished he could at least smile. "Just cleaning up loose ends."

"I think I have it now," she said softly.

"You have what?"

"The voice. Your voice. I can do it now."

He'd forgotten all about her intention to impersonate him.

"Do you want me to do it for you?" she asked.

"Sure, go ahead."

She cleared her throat, then out of the shadows came a deeper voice that jarred him. "Hey, babe, it was great while it lasted. So long, babe."

He didn't realize he was slowing until he felt the car start to lug. Downshifting he said, "That's me?"

"I was just doing you, saying what you would have said to your appointment if she'd shown up."

As he glanced at her, the lights from oncoming cars flashed across her face. Her eyes were dark and her mouth looked tight, and for a brief moment he thought he saw anger there. Then the light was gone, and he was left wondering just who Genna Wade really was.

4

Genna had almost choked on the words from the fax as she'd said them, and she wasn't sure how she'd expected Nick to respond. But she was surprised when he said, "Well, you obviously don't know me, after all."

She wished she felt that way, as if this person was a total stranger to her. But beyond what she knew from Belinda, there was something about him that left her feeling as if they'd met before, as if she'd known him for a very long time. Stupid, foolish rationale, she thought, but she said, "I thought we were getting to know each other."

He was silent for a long moment, then cast her a fleeting glance. "Are we, Doctor?"

Doctor? She cringed at that title when she was going so far afield, but this wasn't professional. This was personal, too personal. And she had to remind herself that Belinda was the one who would suffer, not her, and not Nick, not unless she could get to him. "Yes, actually, I think we are."

"That's good news," he said with a sigh.

She wished she could take back what she'd said to him. It hadn't been smart, but this man tended to make her do less than smart things. "Very good news," she forced herself to say softly as she looked out at the night. The weather was a safe subject until she figured out how to get on with things. "And this evening is beautiful, isn't it?"

"Beautiful," he echoed.

"It's Christmastime and there's a full moon and so many stars."

"Christmas," he murmured. "I'd almost forgotten about it."

"I guess you've got other things on your mind," she said before she realized she was going to say it. "Oh, I'm sorry." This was going from bad to worse. "I just meant that—"

"That I'm single-minded, hardheaded, hard-hitting and shut off. And that means no holidays."

"Does it?"

"Of course it doesn't," he said as he slowed the car. "I'm just not big on holidays."

"Your family doesn't celebrate them?"

"Oh, they celebrate them. Down to and including a world-famous party every Christmas Eve."

"A party? That sounds like fun."

"It's not meant for fun. The definition of a party for the Marsdens is a place to make contacts. The bigger the better. Even though my father's out of the loop on business, he still has political and business connections that he keeps up with at the party."

"So you came by it naturally, didn't you? The business being everything? Being a workaholic?"

"I guess so," he murmured.

"And your mother, how does she put up with all of that?"

"She understands it. She's been around the business for years and knows how important those contacts are for everyone."

Pieces fell into place for Genna, pieces that fit together to make him who and what he was. And she knew that he was more complex than just being self-centered and egotistical. Much more complex. But what she had to do was simple. He would never forget Belinda or what he did to her. She would make sure of that.

"What do you do for the holidays, get together with other psychologists and analyze each other?"

She laughed at that, allowing the humor in an attempt to take the edge off her bunching nerves. "No, not quite."

"Then what do you do?"

"I spend it with family and friends."

"Big meal and that sort of thing?"

"Sure, the meal, the gifts, singing carols, watching favorite movies over and over again."

"Movies?"

"You know, *It's a Wonderful Life* and *Miracle on 34th Street*."

"I think I've heard of them."

"Heard of them? You've never seen them?"

"Sorry, never have." He cast her a quick, dark look, but she could see a smile playing at his mouth. "And don't tell me what that means to me psychologically, okay?"

"I'll give you a Christmas present," she said, and knew she'd taken him aback when the smile was gone and he narrowed his eyes on her.

"What?"

"My present to you—no more analyzing. Okay?"

"I'll gratefully accept that, and now I have to come up with something suitable for your gift," he said. Then, before she could respond, he motioned ahead of them. "There's the restaurant."

She glanced ahead at a Spanish-style building built precariously close to the edge of the bluffs that fringed the highway and overlooked the ocean. A wraparound porch flared out over the water, and small white Christmas lights framed the angles and shapes of the tiled roof.

She'd never been here before, and as she looked back at Nick, she knew there were a lot of places she'd never been, and places she probably shouldn't go. A dangerous man, she admitted to herself, but a man she could handle. She knew she could handle him, do what she planned on doing and get out before things got too complicated.

As he drove toward the front of the restaurant and pulled into the valet parking area, she steeled herself and plunged right ahead. She said things she thought she should say and hated the way they sounded seductive, even in her own words. "I think this all has possibilities, going from strangers to..." Her voice trailed off as she realized just where her thoughts were going. Into places she certainly didn't want to even consider, not with Nick.

"Yes, possibilities," he murmured.

She watched him carefully, trying to read his expression and his shadowy profile. "I just meant that we can see if there...if there's anywhere to go."

"Yes, we can do that," he said as he stopped on the cobbled drive to the restaurant.

"And if things don't work out?" she asked.

He turned to her with the shadow of a smile playing at his lips. "I sincerely hope that isn't the case, but if it is, we just get on with our lives and figure this was just a blip, a could-have-been that wasn't."

"You're very philosophical," she said, wondering just how he would have dealt with Belinda in person? Casually, coolly, firmly. Undoubtedly.

"No, I'm realistic," he said, as the valet opened his door.

Nick turned from her and slipped out, and at the same time her door was opened and she got out into the chilly night air. The scent of Christmas lingered in the air, then she saw bowers of pine garlands strung around the entryway. And both massive doors to the entrance had silver Christmas wreaths decorating them.

"Merry Christmas," the attendant said as he closed the door on the Porsche.

Genna nodded to him, then Nick was there, his hand taking her upper arm. The contact startled her, partly because she hadn't expected it and partly because it was the first time she'd actually felt his touch. Either reason could have explained the way her breath caught and her heart started to speed up. She hoped it was the first reason. She didn't want to deal with the second one.

She moved to the door, slipping ahead of him, and thankfully the contact was broken as they went inside. The interior was dimly lit and reeked of intimacy. Not exactly what she wanted right now even though it would certainly work for what she had to do. Nonetheless, it made her even more nervous and uneasy. The alcohol from the gin gimlets gave her some degree of protection, taking the edge off his closeness.

As she went toward the reservations desk, she didn't have to turn to know where Nick was. She could feel him behind her, then to her left, sensing his heat and his presence. Then a hostess was there, an elegant young blond woman who smiled as they approached her. But as she glanced past Genna, her smile widened and brightened.

"Oh, Mr. Marsden, how nice to see you again. I didn't see you on the books."

"I didn't make reservations, Toni. This is a last-minute thing, but I was hoping you could work us in."

She nodded. "For you, sir, no problem. I'm sure we can get your usual table, if you wouldn't mind waiting for a few minutes?"

Usual table? Genna felt her expression tighten. Of course he knew this place. He had the money to afford it, and the need for privacy with his dates, who obviously numbered a lot.

"I don't need that table. How about something at the back by the windows?" he asked.

She glanced at Genna who felt her face heat slightly at the scrutiny, then back at Nick. "Yes, sir, that's no problem," she said with all but a conspiratorial wink. "I have something available right now. Just follow me."

The man had women eating out of his hand, including this woman. Genna moved quickly to follow the hostess into the main dining area, decorated discreetly for Christmas. They bypassed a polished wood dance area under a huge crystal chandelier, where a man sat at a black concert grand piano playing classical Christmas music.

The hostess led the way to a small alcove on the

far side of the room, to a space that had a single table that took advantage of a sweeping view of the night and the ocean. As Genna sat down in the chair Nick pulled out for her, she heard him say, "The usual and an assortment of appetizers."

"Right away, Mr. Marsden," the woman said, and moved away as Nick took the chair opposite Genna.

Genna looked across the table at Nick and had to concede that this man looked good in any light. In here, in the seductively low glow from the flicker of the candles on the lace and crystal table, he was devastatingly attractive. But the idea that he was just as devastatingly attractive to any woman he came in contact with managed to temper her reaction a bit.

"You come here a lot?" she asked as she reached to slip a pale rose-colored napkin out of a golden ring.

He slipped off his leather jacket, letting it drape back over his chair, then looked at her. "I like it here. The service is great, and I firmly believe that once you find something good, it pays to go back."

She picked up the leather-covered menu, opened it and scanned the perfectly scripted columns. Not a price was in sight, but a lot of French words were in place. "I think this is well out of my price range," she murmured.

A white-coated waiter came right then with a bottle of champagne and two delicate flutes. He smiled at Genna, then nodded at Nick as he carefully poured the bubbly liquid into the crystal. "Merry Christmas, Mr. Marsden."

"Same to you, John," Nick said as he tasted the champagne the waiter offered to him. He nodded, then said, "Very good." As the waiter served Genna, Nick said, "What would you like to eat?"

The idea of any food made her feel peculiarly queasy right then, but she said, "Anything's fine with me."

As Genna sipped from the delicate goblet, Nick ordered without looking at his unopened menu. Genna didn't pay much attention to what he was doing; instead, she let the champagne slip coolly down her throat, shifting to a welcome warmth in her middle.

She fingered the stem of the crystal as she looked away to the night outside, to the line of tiny white lights that framed the windows and the dark ocean beyond. "I am in control," she told herself over and over again. "I am in control." Another drink of champagne, and she felt herself start to settle a bit more.

But as she glanced at Nick's reflection in the window, she knew that neither gin gimlets nor champagne would be enough to kill whatever the man had that touched her. The darkness of the night was his backdrop, and shadows touched his eyes and throat. But he was looking at her, studying her as the waiter left, and she felt a heat growing in her that had no place in this scheme. No place at all.

She quickly looked away, sipped the last of her champagne, and as she put the goblet back on the table, Nick was filling it for her from the towel-draped bottle. Without looking at him, she drank more, letting the coolness trickle down her throat, but it didn't do a thing to kill the heat deep inside her.

When she put the goblet down, surprised to see that it was almost empty again, she had to brace herself to look back at Nick. When she met his gaze, she forced herself to focus on reality. She had no illusions. She knew what this man was and that she was the one who was in control.

He nodded toward her glass. "More?"

She fingered the fragile stem with annoyingly unsteady fingers, and almost refused, but the champagne was helping. It was making that shadowy smile of his less disturbing. She nudged her glass toward him. "Yes, thanks."

He tipped the bottle, letting the amber liquid rise in the goblet. While he poured himself more, she sipped the champagne, then sat back. "I have to admit that you were right," she said.

He looked at her over the rim of his drink, one eyebrow lifting in her direction. "I like being right. But what was I right about?"

"Peace and quiet." She glanced out at the main

section of the restaurant to the piano player who had just started a rendition of "A Merry Little Christmas." "And the music is wonderful."

"Dance?"

She heard the single word, and as it was uttered, images flashed in her mind, disconcerting images of being touched by Nick and held. Just sitting here with him felt seductive. And the idea of dancing was beyond disturbing. Yet how could she seduce him if she never touched him again? She looked at her drink, still held in her hands. "I'm not very good at dancing."

"It's slow, it's easy, and if you step on my toes, I won't yell."

She glanced up at him, the candlelight flickering across his features. For a moment she met his dark gaze and felt herself getting lost in it, then she forced herself to keep eye contact and play the game. "Promise?" she asked softly, hearing the seductive teasing in her own voice.

He saw the flare of awareness in his eyes as he mimed a cross over his heart. "Promise." He stood and looked down at her, then he held out a hand to her with a provocative smile. "How about it?"

She could do this. She knew she could, and she steeled herself as she stood to face him. Control. That's what this was all about. And she had control because she had no illusions about this man at all. She slowly raised her hand to him and almost felt her breath catch when his fingers closed over hers. Strong and sure. Filled with heat. And she felt surrounded by the sensations.

As she let him lead her to the dance floor, she forced herself to focus. She refused to absorb the feeling of his touch on her. When she looked up at him as they stepped onto the dance floor where other couples moved to the slow music, she fixed her mind firmly on what she was doing here. And when he reached out and drew her to him, she told herself that he'd held Belinda like this. He'd spanned her waist with one large hand, gently easing her to him, and had held her against his lean body.

Belinda. Belinda. A mantra against all the feelings that she knew could explode in her if she let down her guard. A mantra against the sensations of his body next to hers, moving with hers; a mantra against that need in her to move even closer to him, to rest her head in the hollow of his shoulder.

A mantra that kept her inches away from him. She closed her eyes against the overwhelming desire to forget everything except the moment. She concentrated on each step she took, on staying in time to the music, but when she felt Nick touch his lips to her hair, she stumbled. Her foot caught, and the next thing she knew, she was up against Nick, his body pressed to hers and his soft laughter rumbling against her breasts.

"I told you, I won't yell," he whispered somewhere near her ear. The heat of his breath against her skin sent a shiver up her spine, and she closed her eyes so tightly that colors exploded behind her lids. "Just move slowly, one, two, three, four." His hand was at the small of her back, and his other hand pulled her hand to his chest. "It's easy."

She tried to laugh, to make herself look up at him and make a joke out of it, but she couldn't. It was all she could do to stay there with him, to make herself move her feet in time with his and not try to get even closer. She took a deep breath, inhaling the scent that clung to him mingled with his body heat, and she made herself keep time. One, two, three, four.

But nothing could disguise that sensation of his body against hers, the way his hips touched hers, the way she could almost feel the beat of his heart against her chin. And just when she wasn't sure she could do it any longer, the music stopped. Nick moved back a bit from her. His hands were gone from her, and when she opened her eyes, he was smiling at her, clapping softly.

"Very good," he murmured.

And her relief at it being over was almost heady. But that relief was short-lived. The man at the piano began another piece, "The Christmas Song," and before she could move back and go to the table, Nick reached out to her again.

His hand took hers, drawing it back to his shoulder, and his other hand touched the small of her back. Then she was being drawn back to him, into his arms, and despite everything in her that screamed for her to not do this again, she found herself going to him.

The next thing she knew she was in his arms, his hips against hers, her breasts pressed to his chest, and as he slowly started to move with her, she felt herself melting against him. Tentatively she touched her cheek to the hollow of his shoulder, and in one flashing moment she had the frightening feeling that she was where she belonged. She was in a place that she'd been looking for all of her life, and the need to get even closer overwhelmed her.

On a professional level she understood Belinda completely. Nick could melt anyone. Just a touch, a look, that scent that clung to him; in combination they were devastating. And it was all she could do to keep reminding herself that she was in control. This was her game, not his, and she was going to win.

5

Nick could feel his breathing catch as Genna came into his arms again. The music drifted around them, but a sense of being isolated with her permeated him. Just her and him. The two of them. A unique experience for him. A truly unique feeling, as unique as the woman herself. He felt her hair tickle his chin as she rested her cheek against his shoulder, and he inhaled the delicate perfume that clung to the silky strands.

He closed his eyes, moving instinctively, needing to absorb whatever was happening, but knowing that if he was like this with her for eternity, he'd never be able to fully absorb the impact of having her in his arms. Impulsively he touched his lips to her hair, and he felt her falter, her steps stumbling for a moment. Then they were in unison again, moving slowly together, hips against hips, and he could feel his body responding in a very obvious way.

As the music ended, he both cursed the ending and was grateful for it. If he had held her like that much longer, he knew what he was feeling would be more than evident for her and everyone to see. He moved back a little, meaning to let her go, to head for the table again, but as she looked up at him from under the veil of lashes, her lips softly parted, he acted on impulse again.

Slowly he framed her face, then did what he knew he'd wanted to do for what seemed forever. He dipped his head toward her, found her lips with his and felt her startled intake of air just as he kissed her. Whatever he had expected from the action, it wasn't for her to stand absolutely still, to make no move at all. And when he drew back, surprised by her lack of response, he found her staring at him as if he was an alien with two heads. Horror, shock, he couldn't place it, but it wasn't lust in her eyes.

He drew back, not sure at all what to do or say, so he didn't say anything. He just touched her elbow, and even though the contact was slight and neutral, he felt her jerk back from it. Then she turned from him, left the dance floor, and just when he thought she was heading for the door to leave, he realized that she was going back to their table.

By the time he got there, she was at the table, drinking the last of her champagne and ignoring the appetizers that had arrived while they'd danced. He slipped into the chair opposite her, silently refilled her champagne flute, then did the same for himself before he put down the bottle and sat back.

Her gaze was on the bubbly liquid, the way the light danced in the effervescence, then she lifted the goblet and he watched her drink half of it. As she put the flute back down, she finally looked at him. Her expression was controlled, much more controlled than he felt right then, but he didn't miss the way her fingers worried the delicate glass stem.

"Do I apologize?" he asked as he reached for a shrimp from the appetizer platter.

Her tongue touched her lips, an action that only further tightened his body, and he shifted forward, the shrimp caught between his fingers, but untouched, as she said, "No."

"Are you angry?" He hated not being able to read her the way he could most people he dealt with. But she wasn't a business person he was trying to better or bluff. At least, he didn't want it to be that way.

"No."

"Upset?"

"No."

"Well, what are you?" he finally asked, nerves making his shoulder muscles tense.

She studied him for a long, disturbing moment, then took the time to sip more of her champagne before she murmured, "Just thinking."

Two could play this game, he thought, and popped the shrimp into his mouth, took his time chewing it, then sipped some of his drink before he sat back and said, "I've caused a lot of different reactions in women, but sending them into a thinking frenzy was never one of them...until now."

"It's no frenzy," she said without a hint of the smile that he'd hoped to produce with his words.

He gave up. He couldn't play this game, whatever that game was. "What's going on, Genna?"

She glanced at her almost-empty glass, then back at him as she pushed the goblet in his direction. "I'm thirsty."

If he tried for a million years, he couldn't act as if that kiss hadn't happened, but that's just what she was doing. And as he refilled her glass, he decided that he wouldn't let her do that. He put the bottle back in the sleeve and sat back. "If you didn't want me to kiss you, I apologize. I thought...I assumed after the dance that things were all right."

She drank more champagne, then looked right at him. "Things?"

"This. You and me. Here. Dancing. Talking." He had to fight not to get closer to her, to try and figure her out. "Things."

She actually smiled at that, a jarring expression that threw him slightly off balance. "Things," she echoed.

He exhaled. "Okay, Doctor. Go ahead."

"With what?" she asked with slightly widened eyes.

"Analyze me. Figure out why I did that. What

drives me to dance with a beautiful woman, to want to kiss her, then what makes me have to know what's going on in her head?" He found his own smile, albeit a wry one. "Explain that to me."

She looked down at her drink, then shook her head. "I gave you a present and I meant it." She smoothed her hair at her ears and he was fascinated to see that her hand was slightly unsteady. "No more analyzing. But I can give you a suggestion."

He glanced at the appetizer tray, but he didn't reach for any more. "Fair enough. Suggest away."

"Control."

"What?"

"You like control. You want to be in control. You don't like not having control."

She was more right than he cared to admit. Not having control drove him crazy. And he felt as out of control with Genna as he ever had with anyone or anything in his life. Except maybe Mars. But that was an entirely different story. "Control," he repeated. "Yes, I like control. Don't you?"

She seemed slightly taken aback by that question. Hesitating, she finally said, "Everyone does."

"*But,*" he said with emphasis, "I don't consider a kiss as a way of getting control."

She studied him for a long moment. "What is a kiss?"

"Two people, mouths touching, pleasure." Extreme pleasure. "A biological phenomenon."

Genna drank the last of her champagne, and was thankful for the building muzziness from the alcohol. It made looking at Nick easier, and it took the edges off her reaction to his kiss. Something she desperately wanted. If she didn't keep up her guard, she could almost feel his lips against hers still. She could almost taste him, and she kept herself from touching her tongue to her lips to see if his taste was still lingering there.

"A biological phenomenon," she repeated. Not even close for her. A totally compelling response that she'd had to fight to keep from giving in to. A kiss that was unlike any other kiss she'd ever experienced. "Whatever."

She needed more champagne, and as if Nick had read her mind, he reached across and finished off the bottle by draining it into her goblet. Nick, reading her mind? The idea was frightening. If he could read her mind, he'd be as shocked as she was with herself. She was out for revenge, not out to have a good time, to have a man smile at her and turn her bones to water or touch her and make her weak. Or kiss her and— She cut off that thought before it had time to fully form.

Quickly she took another drink and spoke as she looked down into her glass. "I guess the bottom line is that we hardly know each other. I'm not used to kissing someone when they're...they're..." She stumbled over the word. What was Nick? A heel?

A user? An egocentric jerk? Or a sexy man? A man who had something that drew her like a moth to a flame?

"A stranger," he finished for her with a touch of exasperation. "Hell, I thought we were past that."

They were, she thought, but kept that to herself. She felt as if she'd known Nick a long time, and she'd never responded to a stranger like she did to him. And that scared her. "We just met," she said with what she hoped was sound logic.

A muffled ringing sound was jarring, and Nick turned, reaching into the pocket of his leather jacket. Then he turned back with a cell phone that he spoke into. "What is it?" he asked abruptly.

He listened for a long moment, then said, "Eileen, go ahead and agree to it. Tomorrow at nine." Then he flipped the phone shut and laid it on the table. "Sorry about that." He fingered the slim phone. "That business appointment—"

A reprieve. And she needed it badly to regroup her strategy with Nick. "I understand. Business. Let's go," she said, and didn't realize how foolish she'd been to mix drinks until she tried to stand. The world shifted for her, and she slowly sank down into the chair again. "Whoa, I'm sorry," she murmured, one hand pressed to the tabletop.

"We don't have to go," he said. "I had the nine o'clock appointment rescheduled for nine tomorrow morning at the offices." He tapped the phone. "I didn't think he'd agree to it, but the man isn't much of a bluffer, after all.''

She realized Nick was looking at her, but when she glanced up at him he was slightly blurry to her, or maybe there were two of him. No, not that, she thought with horror. She couldn't cope with one Nick. Two would be impossible. She tried to focus both her eyes and her thoughts. He'd said something about business, about tomorrow morning. "I'm...I'm sorry, the call...?"

He shook his head and she wished he hadn't. It only made the whole world feel more unsteady for her. "It's nothing. Just business. And it's settled. I have to meet him at nine tomorrow morning in my office."

"Did you fax him?" she heard herself asking, horrified that she was saying things that she wasn't even thinking about first.

"Fax? No, Eileen called him."

"Eileen. And Eileen is...?"

"My assistant."

She wished she could center herself, instead she found herself just repeating what he said. "Oh, your assistant."

"She prefers that to secretary."

"Secretary," she murmured as she picked up the goblet again and drank the last of it.

"She's been with me for years," he said.

"Years."

"I think you need to eat something," he said.

She realized that he was frowning at her. "What?"

"Food. You had a couple of drinks at the Century Club and the champagne here, but you need food."

She looked down at the appetizer tray, and her stomach revolted. "No, no food," she whispered. "I...I don't usually drink and I...I think I need some...some fresh air."

She hadn't realized she was standing until she saw Nick coming toward her, his hand out, then he was touching her. An anchor, that's what he was. His hand on her arm was holding her steady, keeping her from just falling into nothingness. "Come on," he was saying. "Let's go for a drive. We can eat in a while."

The waiter was there, watching them, something in his hands. But he didn't hesitate when Nick said, "We're leaving. Just put that on my account."

"Yes, sir," he said.

"And have my car brought around."

"Yes, sir," he said again, then was gone and it was just Nick and Genna and music, a soft version of "Greensleeves." Nick had his arm around her shoulder, and she was walking with him, although she felt as if she was moving in slow motion. Someway they'd made it out of the restaurant, and they were in the parking lot. The Porsche seemed to come out of nowhere, screeching to a halt, then Genna was being eased into the car.

She closed her eyes, snuggling into the leather seat, but Nick's voice drew her. "Genna? Genna?"

Opening her eyes, she found Nick right there, so close she could feel his breath on her face. "Nick," she murmured.

"Yes, it's me. I think it's better if I just take you home."

"I guess so," she said, then realized that she was reaching up to Nick, her fingers touching his jaw. "I wish..." She sighed deeply. "No, I don't wish..."

"What I wish is for you to tell me where you live. I'll drive you home, then arrange for your car to be taken there for you."

She looked into eyes so blue they looked like the ocean, and they were just as hypnotic to her. Her fingers felt warm where they touched him, and she wished that he'd kiss her again. One more time.

"Genna, what's your address?" she heard him ask, his voice echoing oddly around her.

"I don't know you well enough," she whispered, staring at his lips. "I wish I did...or maybe I don't..."

"Genna, love, where do you live?"

Dammit all, she thought, the doctor is drunk. Very drunk, and just on a little champagne and gin. No, not a little. But she couldn't remember how many glasses she'd had of anything. Or when she'd eaten last, or when she'd realized that dealing with Nick wasn't going to be as easy as she'd thought it would be.

"Genna?" he was saying softly. "Genna?"

Oh, God, that voice. Smooth and rough at the same time. Silky and harsh combined. Sexy. She pushed that away, but it wouldn't go. Sexy. Dammit. So sexy. No wonder women fell all over him, begging him to... That thought definitely was pushed away, and as she shoved at it with all of her will, she closed her eyes again. If she didn't look at him, maybe she stood a chance of getting out of this without too much damage.

She heard him say, "Okay, love, we'll figure this out," then she let herself slide into a nice soft place where she didn't have to think about anything.

Nick looked at Genna, snuggled into the seat, her cheek resting against the side and her lashes fanned on her delicate skin. Beautiful. Beautiful and drunk. He smiled at that. An easy drunk, that was for sure. He sat in the car for a long moment, just watching her, then let himself brush her cheek with the tips of his fingers.

She sighed deeply, then settled even more, and he drew back. As he shifted in the seat, he saw her purse on the floor by her feet and reached for it. He slipped out a thin wallet, opened it and found her driver's license. Genna Marie Wade, a San Francisco address, an emergency number in the Bay area. Twenty-nine years old, and the picture on the license didn't do any justice to the reality of the woman.

He put the wallet back, then slipped the car into gear and drove off. He could go back to the Century Club and see if there was a local address in her car, but as he drove onto the highway, he realized that he didn't even know what her car looked like. Much less where she'd parked it. When she sighed, he glanced at her in the dim lights from the dash. There was only one thing to do.

As he got to the intersection, he turned away from the direction of the Century Club. Instead, headed for the coast and his new apartment on the top floor of one of the best residential buildings near the beach. By the time he turned into the underground parking at the building, Genna had settled into a deep sleep, and the silence in the car was broken only by a few soft sighs that ran riot over Nick's nerves.

He couldn't stop a part of him that wished she was awake and sober and going willingly to his place with him. He couldn't think of anything he'd like more than to spend the night with Genna, and another thought came that he'd never considered before. He'd like to wake with her, turn over and see her face near his in the coolness of morning light. That was odd. He never thought of more than the moment with women. But tonight was a night of firsts for him.

He drove through the underground parking area for the twenty-story apartment building, slipped into his parking spot and got out. When he opened the passenger door, he crouched down and gently eased Genna up and into his arms. He nudged the door shut with his foot and headed for the private elevator to the top floor.

Despite all of his good intentions of just carrying her up to the apartment and settling her there until she was sober enough to give him an address, it didn't work that way. Nothing about this evening had worked the way he'd thought it would.

She snuggled into him, pressing her face to his chest and resting a hand over his heart through the leather jacket. Quickly he shifted her so he could enter the code for his floor, then as the doors slid shut he saw himself in the mirrors that lined the car.

Instead of being in a tense, mean-spirited meeting, he was carrying a woman up to his apartment, a woman who stirred him on a basic level that he'd rarely experienced before. When she shifted and her hand came up to go around his neck while she got closer to him, his body tightened.

He wished his housekeeper was here instead of taking off the four days for the holiday. At least Myra could have helped him get her settled and given him a buffer against whatever it was that drew him to her. But he was going to have to get her into bed, then back off and leave her alone.

"A noble man," he muttered to himself.

"Mmmmmm?" The soft sound startled him, and as he looked down at her, her eyes fluttered open. "Nick?"

"Yes, it's me."

She smiled slightly, as if there had been a joke he wasn't included in. "It is you," she whispered thickly, then her eyes drifted closed and she rubbed her cheek against his chest.

"Genna?" he said, but there was no response this time at all.

Dammit all, he should have just kept driving until she came around. He shouldn't have brought her up here, because he knew that what he was feeling right then wasn't even close to being noble.

6

Nick reached for the button of the elevator to go back down, but before he could manage to get his hand near the panel, the door opened up to the foyer of his apartment. He'd only been in the place for two months and it was sparsely furnished to say the least. Stark, that's what it was.

Only a mirror hung on the off-white walls in the two-level entry space. A sweeping staircase to the right led up to the balcony off the master bedroom suite that held only a bed and dresser. In the step-down living space right ahead, the hardwood floors were bare, and no drapes hung on the floor-to-ceiling windows to hide the city and ocean views. Getting furniture to fill the place hadn't been high on his priority list, except for his office off the kitchen.

He stood very still for a moment in a place that had never felt like home, then started to turn, ready to leave, but he heard a door open and close deep in the apartment. His housekeeper should have left hours ago, but he was glad she hadn't. "Myra?" he called out.

He heard footsteps on the hardwood floor in the hallway near the office, then Eileen came walking out into the foyer. "No, it's not Myra. She left when she let me in. I was just getting the papers you'll need for—"

Her words were cut off when she came into the foyer, and her eyes widened. "Oh, boy, I am sorry. I had no idea you'd have—"

"Eileen, it's not what you think. I went to the Century Club to meet with the stewardess—"

"I know you told me everything was going to be fine, that there were no problems," she said, cutting off his explanation. "But I think you've gone a bit too far. I had no idea that under that button-down shirt was a man capable of—of this." She dropped the purse and coat she'd been carrying onto the bottom step of the staircase, then came closer and stared at a motionless Genna. "My God, what did you do to the poor girl? Give her knockout drops or poison her?"

He almost laughed at that. "No, she just mixed drinks with champagne."

"You had champagne with your brother's ex-girlfriend?"

"No, she isn't the stewardess."

She looked up at Nick. "Then just who is she,

and why is she so drunk you had to carry her up here?"

"It's a long story, and right now I want to get her to bed."

She put up both hands, palms out. "Whoa, there. I don't want to even go near that statement. It's not my problem, none of my business."

"I mean, I need to get her into bed so she can sober up."

She looked at Genna again and shook her head. "Now that I look at her, she's really not your brother's type, is she?"

She wasn't any type. Just the most fascinating woman he'd ever met. "She's got nothing to do with Mars. But since you're here, you can help me. I'll take her upstairs and you can come up and make her comfortable for the night."

"That *definitely* isn't in my job description."

"Consider your contract revised," Nick murmured.

"This I would have expected from Mars, but not from you, boss. You know, I've always hoped that you'd loosen up a bit, but bringing home a drunk woman and putting her in your bed is just a bit much, don't you think?"

"That's enough, Eileen," he said. "I could use some coffee, if you wouldn't mind making me some."

"Another amendment to my contract," she muttered as she turned and headed back toward the kitchen area. "Coffee coming right up."

As Nick started up the stairs with Genna, he called after Eileen. "Come on up as soon as you can."

"Yes, sir," she called back, and Nick ignored the touch of mocking sarcasm in her voice.

Genna felt herself moving, gently cradled into heat and strength. She was drunk, she knew that, and now she was imagining she was being carried. It was her illusion, and in that illusion, she knew it was Nick carrying her. He was taking her with him, upward, into quiet darkness, his arms around her, his breath brushing her hair as he moved.

And she held to him, relishing the way her drunken imagination could fabricate the intricate fantasy of his scent, that clean soapiness, mingling with the night and leather and a certain maleness that clung to him. She even contrived the feel of leather against her cheek and under her palms. A heart beat near her ear, the steady thumping a perfect rhythm to go with her breathing.

Maybe if she drank more she would have passed it all off as ordinary, but it felt so extraordinary and so right. Nick holding her. Nick carrying her. Then she felt them stop, and he was putting her down into softness. But she didn't want him to leave her. And it was her dream, her illusion, so she reached out for him. She felt his hand under hers, his fingers lacing with hers, and she managed to open her eyes just a bit.

There were shadows everywhere, a surreal glow from somewhere off in the distance, and Nick over her. Her tongue felt uncooperative and she was beginning to feel a vague aching sensation behind her eyes. A dream that was shifting without her being able to control it. Then Nick was coming closer to her, speaking to her, his breath brushing her face with heat.

"The good doctor is drunk," he said softly.

Her tongue touched her lips, then she whispered, "The good doctor...is...very drunk." She swallowed and moved her hand from his to reach up and touch his jaw. The dream was so real she could feel the slight bristling of a new beard, the heat of his skin. "Very...very..." she whispered.

"Yes, very," he breathed.

"You, too," she said in a slightly breathless voice as her finger trailed along the line of his jaw to touch his full bottom lip. "Very...very..."

He covered her hand with his, pinning it against his cheek and relishing the way it felt there. "Very what?" he asked softly.

She smiled up at him, a man blurred by the shadows and the fantasy that was being woven. "Very tempting," she said honestly. "Very tempting."

"Well, that has possibilities," he breathed, coming even closer.

She remembered the dance, the way he'd looked at her, and she knew where this dream came from. That need she'd felt when he'd touched her. "You...you kissed me, didn't you?" she asked, her words vaguely slurred.

"Yes, Doctor, I did."

Her hand moved from his, and she slowly slid it around the back of his neck, the feel of his skin very real in the dream. "I owe you...for that," she said, wishing she could control her words in the dream instead of them coming in breathless gasps.

"You owe me what?"

"This." And she tugged at him, bringing him down to her, then her lips found his.

Even in the dream, a passion for this man came from nowhere, exploding into fire, suddenly there, all around her, coursing through him and consuming her. Her lips parted in invitation, and he was over her, his weight on her before she realized it. His tongue teased her, his hands touched her, and the dream became exquisite pleasure for her.

He explored her, invaded her, and she yearned toward him. Her arms circled his neck, her breasts straining against his chest, and her response to him was swift and sure. This wasn't right. The dream was wrong. She was supposed to be seducing him. Not like this.

But a softness that hovered around her started pressing in on her. She felt his hands at her blouse, then the silk was gone and he touched her breasts. The moan sounded so real, her moan of pleasure as his fingers found her nipple through the thin lace of her bra. Too real. As real as an ache deep inside her that this man had produced.

When the softness came closer and closer, she knew that if she fought it, this dream would go into territory that even a dream shouldn't explore. Not with Nick. Not when this was all wrong. As his lips pressed to her exposed throat, she felt herself slipping. Drifting. Going into a muzziness that blocked all thought and reason. And as she let go, the last thing she thought was if things had been different, she would have wished this wasn't a dream. Then it was all gone.

"Good God, Nicholas!" Nick heard from behind him.

He looked down at Genna, at her eyes closing, her body going limp in his hold. She'd slipped back into sleep, but not before testing him to the limit, drawing a response from him that was more than physically evident. He eased back from her, but didn't take his eyes off her.

"And I thought you meant it, that you just wanted her to sleep it off!"

He stayed sitting on the bed, not about to stand so Eileen could see just how far he'd let himself go. "I meant it, but—" He took a shaky breath. "She kissed me," he said and knew how lame that sounded.

Eileen was at the other side of the bed, and he could feel her staring at him. "Boss, she's drunk."

"I know. I know." He turned to his right, standing with his back to Eileen. "Make her comfortable. There's some T-shirts in the dresser. I'll be downstairs," he muttered, then left.

Nick stood by the windows in the living room and stared out at the night, at the flashing of Christmas lights far below, and even to the red and green lights on the boats anchored in the marina on the coast. He'd never done that before, he'd never even dreamed of taking advantage of a woman, but he'd come close. Too damned close. And when he heard Eileen come down the stairs, he was ready for her anger.

He wasn't ready for her to stand in the entryway and say, "All tucked in. I'm leaving."

He turned and saw her across the room. "She's settled in?"

"Safe and sound." She hesitated, then said, "Look, it's none of my business, but are you all right?"

He nodded. "I'm fine. It's just been a crazy night. First the stewardess didn't show, then—"

"You never even talked to the Hogan woman?"

"She called it off, said that we just had to get on

with things. She backed off. Then Ron called off the meeting, and I met Genna—"

"Genna?"

"Genna Wade, my guest."

"If I had time I'd ask where you met and how and why she's so drunk, but I don't have the time or the energy." She crossed to the bottom step to get her purse and coat, then went to the elevator and pushed the Down button. The doors opened immediately and she got in, turning to look back at Nick.

"I've got your notes. The meeting's at nine. Don't be late. And say hello to your friend for me." As she reached for the inside button, she said, "You could use some furniture in this place, you know."

"I know."

"And put up something for Christmas. Maybe some tinsel or mistletoe."

He nodded as the door shut, then he stood alone in the huge, empty room, and all he could think about was Genna in his bed upstairs. Without looking at the staircase, he went into the kitchen, found the fresh coffee, poured himself a cup. Then he went in search of some sheets and blankets to make a bed on the couch in his office.

Genna woke with a raging headache, a mouth that felt as if cotton had been stuffed in it and a terrible sense that something was very wrong. Then she opened her eyes, sat up and knew just how wrong everything was.

She was in a bedroom she'd never seen before, looking out a window that had a view she knew she'd never looked at before, and she was wearing a T-shirt she had never owned before. She sat very still, thinking, trying to focus. Then one word came to her. *Nick.*

She looked at the other side of the bed, thankful to find it undisturbed, but that still didn't answer any of the questions that bombarded her. She looked around, saw her clothes on a side table by the huge, four-poster, dark wood bed, and she could tell all she was wearing was her panties and the plain white T-shirt.

She swallowed hard when sickness rose in her throat. This was wrong, all wrong, and the sickness attacked her with a vengeance when she remembered last night. The dance, the kiss, being drunk and that dream. Dammit all, it wasn't a dream. She was here with Nick. She knew she was, yet she couldn't remember anything beyond him kissing her and her responding.

She was supposed to be in control. She was supposed to be the one calling the shots. She pushed back the linen, swung her legs over the side of the bed, then got out onto the cold wooden floors. She took a moment to steady herself when the world began to undulate, then as it settled, she looked around the room. A plain, sparsely decorated room, with no pictures, just the fantastic view of the ocean.

She listened for a moment, but couldn't hear a sound. Then she saw an open door and what looked like a dressing room beyond it. She crossed the wooden floor and stepped into a walk-through closet lined with suits on one side, shirts on the other and shoes neatly paired on holders on the floor.

She took one breath and remembered that scent clinging to Nick, filling her senses when he'd been carrying her. Yes, he'd carried her. She remembered vaguely that feeling and decided not to think about it. She went through the closet and stepped into a white-on-white marble bathroom suite, with a sunken tub, a huge shower stall and wraparound windows that exposed a full city view.

She went to the sink, took several drinks of cool water, then looked in the gilded mirror over the freestanding vanity. Her hair was tumbled around her slightly pale face, and all makeup was a thing of the past. She stared at herself as if she could make herself remember what had happened, but she drew a blank. And that made her stomach clench again. Doctor Genna Wade, thinking she could get revenge on a man like Nicholas Marsden. Instead she'd ended up drunk in his apartment, and God knew what had happened here.

She quickly washed her face, brushed her hair back from her face and decided it was time to face

Nick and get this over with. But as she walked back through the closet, literally holding her breath to keep from inhaling his scent, she couldn't help but feel that if they'd made love, she would remember. Could a woman ever forget being touched by a man like Nick?

Then her stomach did major loops. If she'd slept with Nick, how could she ever face Belinda? How could she ever face herself again? She walked faster through the bedroom and opened the door to step out onto an inside balcony that overlooked a spacious entryway with what looked like an elevator door instead of a regular entry door.

She went along the balcony, down the steps and onto the cool flooring. She looked around at an all but empty space. Not even carpets. Just hardwood flooring and views. That was it. She couldn't hear anything and finally got up the nerve to call out, "Nick?"

Her voice echoed in the space, but no one was there. Then she caught the aroma of coffee brewing and headed toward it. She went down a short hallway and through an arched doorway into a kitchen that was as Spartan as the rest of the house. None of it looked lived in. She spotted the coffeemaker across the white tiled floor and crossed to it. As she reached for the pot, she saw a piece of paper on the granite counter by it and saw her name scrawled at the top. She picked it up.

Genna,
I knew you'd be needing coffee. I had a meeting at nine, and I'll be back as soon as I can. Make yourself comfortable, food's in the walk-in refrigerator. I'll see you soon.

Then a scrawl that she recognized from the fax at the bottom of it.

She poured herself a cup of coffee, found a banana in the refrigerator, then turned and saw a door on the far wall partially ajar. She went over to it, and as she opened the door farther, she found a room that didn't look as if it belonged there.

An office. Cabinets were lined up under a bank of windows. Shelves on two full walls. A telephone and fax machine to one side, stacked papers and a computer on a desk with a leather high-backed chair behind it. A workaholic. The only room with any touch of humanity was where he worked. And a part of Genna felt a twinge of sadness at a life so ruled by work and achievement. The sadness lasted until she remembered why she was here and what she needed to find out.

She saw the fax machine, then knew she wasn't staying to wait for Nick. That she wouldn't do. If they had slept together, she needed to get herself under control. And if they hadn't slept together, she had to regroup. This wasn't going the way she'd hoped it would. But from now on she was in control.

She took a sheet of paper from a stack near the fax, wrote quickly on it, then put it in the machine. Just when she was going to call for the number, she spotted a speed dial list by the machine. His office at Marsden was the first one on the list, the fax line the second. She quickly put in the number, then watched it feed through the machine. As soon as she knew it had been sent, she turned from the fax and left the room to get dressed and get out of Nick's apartment.

Nick walked out on the meeting with Weiss just fifteen minutes after it started. He strode out of the conference room, down the hallway and into his office. Closing the door firmly behind him, he wondered why he'd bothered insisting on the meeting at all. The man was impossible, and the merger probably wouldn't go through, anyway.

It frustrated him and angered him. If he'd known Weiss was going to be so difficult, he would have stayed at the apartment to talk to Genna. To see her in the morning. Then he smiled. Hung over in the morning, but he thought it would still be an improvement over what he'd just gone through.

Then he thought of last night and he knew there wouldn't be a comparison. Right then he knew that he was going to do something he never would have done before he met Genna. He was going home. He was getting out of here, instead of doing what he would have done just yesterday. He wasn't going to wait here to outbluff Weiss. He had done what he had to do with Weiss, now he was out of here.

But before he could ring for Eileen, she was knocking on the door and coming into the office. It was déjà vu, her coming toward him holding out a sheet of paper to him. But this time she wasn't grimacing the way she had last night with the first fax from the Hogan woman. Now she was smiling as if she was in on a joke that Nick didn't have a clue about.

"What's going on?"

"This is for you," she said, holding the paper out to him. "A fax. From Ms. Wade."

He took it from her. "Genna faxed me?"

"Take a look."

He looked down at the single sheet and knew why Eileen was smiling. In very neat handwriting Genna wrote:

Nick,
I can't sit here and wait for you to get back. I've got things to do, so I'll be in touch with you later on today.

Genna.

Nick glanced at the banner on top of the paper, and any hopes of getting her fax number off it were dashed when he saw his own banner from his home office on the paper. "When did this come in?" he asked Eileen.

"Just a few minutes ago. She must have sobered up."

"It seems so," he said, and knew that he wasn't leaving the office after all. He had nowhere he wanted to be anymore. He circled the desk, sank down in his chair and dropped the note on the desktop. He had no address, no phone number and no idea who she was visiting in L.A. For once Nick felt at a loss, and he didn't like that feeling at all. Not any more than he liked the feeling that he'd be marking time until he heard from Genna again.

7

Genna spent the day fighting a horrible headache, furiously cleaning up Belinda's apartment and trying not to think about what might have, or might not have, happened with Nick. But taking aspirins and keeping busy just weren't enough to stop the thoughts that beat against her.

Even when the entire apartment was cleaner and more orderly than it had been since Belinda moved in, the unknown weighed heavily on her. And she knew that she had to find out what really happened.

Nick was becoming an obsession for her, and she understood more and more how Belinda could have been so taken with him. But the longer she waited to contact him and find out what happened last night, the more she felt guilty and stupid. A psychologist who had allowed herself to get drunk, to kiss a man, to practically offer herself to him, or who possibly *had* offered herself to him. A man her best friend loved, or thought she loved. It made her feel vaguely sick and increased the pounding in her head.

Finally, when she couldn't stand it anymore, she made herself take the next step and contact Nick. She found the number for his office and placed the call. It took over two minutes just to get to Nick's office phone. Then she was put on hold by a lady. When the phone was finally picked up by Nick, when she heard him say, "Nicholas Marsden," she almost hung up. But she didn't.

Taking a shaky breath, she managed, "Nick, it's Genna."

"Genna." Just the way he said her name made her uneasy. "How are you doing?"

"I'm fine."

"That's good." He hesitated. "I wish you'd waited for me to get back."

"I had things to do."

"Speaking of things to do, how about doing dinner? But this time we actually eat." She heard his soft chuckle, and heat flooded her face. If she'd made love to Nick, wouldn't she remember? Wouldn't there be something left, something she could pull up and know it had been real. "I'm hungry, how about you?"

She could stop it right here, but she knew she wouldn't. She couldn't. She needed to know for herself, and she still hadn't done a thing to help Belinda. If anything, she'd probably done more to hurt

Belinda than she ever had in her life. "Yes, sure," she murmured.

"Good, give me your address and I'll come to get you."

"No, I'll meet you. Just tell me where."

"You need to get your car from the Century Club, so why not—"

"I got it this morning," she said quickly.

"Okay, then where would you like to go?"

Someplace not so intimate, not like the place they'd been last night. No dancing, no soft music, no candles and no champagne. "Do you know where the Santa Monica Pier is?"

"I can find it."

"There are benches right by the drinking fountains, past the carousel and the hot-dog concessions. I'll be there in an hour."

"Okay, I'll see you there in an hour."

She hung up and sank slowly down onto the wicker-and-loose-cushion couch by the phone. She needed a safe meeting, if there was such a thing with Nick, so she could sort things out. Being out in the open by the beach with a chilly breeze coming in off the water sounded as if it was about as safe as she could get right now. At least, she hoped it would be safe.

Genna sat on the benches by the closed carousel and squinted into the setting sun. A cool breeze off the ocean ruffled her loose hair and filtered through the loose sweater and jeans she was wearing with suede boots. She heard the motor of the Porsche before she turned and saw Nick parking in the lot behind her by the closed hot-dog stands. The car slipped into a parking spot, then the motor was silenced and she saw Nick step out.

He looked as if he had come directly from the office, dressed in a gray three-piece suit and was loosening his tie as he glanced around. As formally dressed as she was casually dressed. Then he spotted her, and even from a distance she felt the impact of his gaze when it met hers. It was all she could do to keep looking at him and lift a hand in acknowledgment. But she didn't stand. She stayed sitting as he strode through the last rays of light from the setting sun toward her.

She never looked away until he was in front of her, standing over her, and she had to tilt her head back to look up at him. "You found it," she said.

"No problem." He glanced around, then back to her. "So, are you ready to go to dinner?"

She couldn't eat, not yet. She made herself stand, making very sure not to touch him as she turned slightly to the view of the beach near the pier. "I'm not really hungry yet. Can we walk for a bit?"

"Walk?" he asked as if it were a foreign word to him.

"You know," she said as she turned back to him. "What poor people do. Use their feet. Walk."

He smiled at that, an expression that rocked her. "I know what walking is."

"Good," she murmured as she turned and started toward the boardwalk by the shops all decorated for the holidays.

He fell in step beside her, but she didn't look at him, as they stepped onto the broad concrete walkway and headed south. She kept her face lifted to the breeze and concentrated on staring straight ahead at the thinning crowds strolling past.

"Can I ask where we're walking to?" he asked.

"Just walking." She inhaled the pungent air. "I...I thought we could talk some more."

"What about?"

"I owe you an apology," she said, keeping her eyes on the horizon.

"An apology?"

"After what happened, I...I'm just embarrassed."

"Why? It happens. People are human. No apologies are needed, believe me."

Oh, God, they *had* slept together. She closed her eyes tightly and swallowed hard before she veered toward a low sea wall that boarded the expansive beach and stepped over it. Bending down, she slipped off her boots and socks, then pressed her feet into the cool dampness of the sand.

"It's just I don't...I mean, I never actually do

anything like that. I mean, we hardly know each other."

"What better way to get to know each other?" he murmured as he stepped over the wall, and she saw his polished oxfords sink in the clinging sand.

This went from bad to worse. And she needed space, not closeness with Nick. She pushed her socks into her boots, then looped her boots on her fingers and started across the sand to the water's edge. She lifted her face, letting the wind stir her hair, and she almost jumped out of her skin when she heard Nick speak from right beside her.

"Don't you think we know each other a bit better now?"

She looked down at her bare feet pressing into the wet sand and at Nick's shoes inches from her. "Better? I...I hardly think that qualifies as getting acquainted," she muttered, hating the heat that she knew was rising in her cheeks and thankful for the failing light.

"I don't know any other way that's quite so intimate as nursing someone through a spell of being drunk."

She turned to him. "What?"

"Drunk. You got drunk. You mixed your drinks."

"I was drunk?"

"You didn't have a hangover?"

"A hangover? Yes, but I thought...I was at your place, in your bed."

He studied her with narrowed eyes, then that smile came again, and this time she could literally feel her heart lurch in her chest. "Oh, so that's what this is all about? You thought that we...that you and I..."

"No, of course not, but I was drunk, and—"

"That doesn't do anything for a guy's ego. You don't remember if we—"

"We didn't do it, did we?" she blurted out.

He moved back to avoid a wave that lapped higher on the sand, while she let the cool water flow around her ankles. He was silent, the coming night making shadows at his jaw and eyes. "It?" he murmured. "Define *it?*"

She turned from him, needing to stop whatever was going on even when he wasn't touching her at all. She stared out across the water at the last tinge of rose and copper in the sky. "Did we or didn't we?"

"What do you want me to say? You were drunk. You wouldn't give me an address to drive you home. I took you to my apartment and let you sleep it off."

She closed her eyes tightly. "You put me to bed?"

"I was going to, but my assistant was there and

she put you to bed. She's the one who put the T-shirt on you. Does that cover everything?''

Not even close. The dream about kissing him, of him on top of her, his hands on her. "That...that was it?"

"That was it...more or less."

"More or less?"

"Okay, less. Is that what you wanted to hear?"

She wanted to hear that she'd just been dreaming, that she'd never been in his bed with him. "I'm just not used to drinking at all, and I haven't been drunk since college."

"A college drunk? I can see why you're worried. Let me assure you that you didn't walk naked on a ledge twenty stories above the city."

Thank goodness she could feel a smile starting at his words. "Naked on a ledge? Don't tell me that you—"

"I won't. Things like that are better left alone," he said.

It was then that she could turn to look at him, a man who was inches from her, the breeze off the Pacific ruffling his hair. And she didn't understand why the knowledge that last night had all been an illusion gave her a touch of disappointment that made no sense at all. "Yes, things are better left alone," she repeated.

He pushed back the sides of his jacket and tucked his hands in the pockets of his perfectly tailored slacks. "Now that we have everything settled, I'm hungry."

Miraculously, so was she. She tucked her hair behind her ears and nodded. "I am, too."

"Good. Let's go."

"Okay, but let me choose."

"Sure."

She headed back to the sea wall and stepped over it, then Nick was by her on the walkway heading for his car. "Can we leave your car here?"

"I didn't bring it," she said. "I walked. There's a place just down the coast that I like." She turned to Nick, who stopped right by her. "How about it?"

"You seem to know this area. Just tell me where we're going."

"Okay," she said, and went to the Porsche. Nick was there, reaching around her to open the door, and that sense of finally being in control was threatened when she felt his shoulder press against hers and his hand cover hers on the handle. As she drew back and brushed at the sand on her feet, he opened the door, then she quickly got inside. When he was behind the wheel and pulling away from the curb, she said, "Just go south," as she managed to put her socks and boots back on.

Nick pulled into traffic on the coast road, and Genna settled back in the seat. "How did the meeting go this morning?" she asked.

"It's gone. More games and manipulations. I walked out."

"The guy sounds either very brave or very stupid," she said. A bit like herself dealing with Nick. "Do you think he was trying to bluff?"

"He is. But I'm not sure he knows when to hold or when to fold. That bothers me. Negotiating is one thing, but destroying your chances doesn't figure."

"Burning bridges?" she asked, looking over at him in the failing light.

"It's an old adage, but true. Never burn your bridges."

"Except in relationships?"

He stayed in the right lane heading down the coast. "What does that mean?"

"When a relationship's over, you get past it."

"What makes you say that?"

"Last night you said you were taking care of things, a woman, and I assumed it was a bad relationship."

"It was," he said without hesitating. "A bridge well burned."

She looked away and out the window, her whole being tightening at his words. Every time it came up, she caught glimpses of a callous man, a man who had little if anything in common with the way he was acting around her. But she knew that when he decided it was over, he'd cut her off just as he had Belinda. But she was going to be the one to cut him off. She wouldn't give him a chance.

"Genna?"

He'd been talking to her, and she didn't have a clue what he'd been saying. "I'm sorry?" she responded.

"I was just reminding you that we made a deal that we wouldn't talk about each other's past mistakes."

She clasped her hands in her lap and looked ahead. "Absolutely. You're right."

"Good," he said on a sigh. "Now, where are we going?"

"South."

"You said that. But do you have a name for the restaurant?"

"It's not a restaurant," she said.

"I thought we were going to eat?"

"We are, but not in a restaurant."

"Okay, I give up. Where are we going?"

A safe place, she thought, a very safe place. Where a man like Nicholas Marsden would be right out of his element and less dangerous. Where she'd have some control. "Right there," she said, and pointed ahead at a glow from the main marina, where a slow stream of cars funneled into the parking areas on the street and parking lots on the opposite side of the water.

"What is it?"

"The best Christmas show in California, probably this side of the Rockies."

"A show?"

"It's a boat parade of lights for the holidays."

He slowed and pulled into a parking spot near a side street and turned off the Porsche. "Okay, a show. Fine. How about food?"

She looked at Nick, knowing this had been a good idea with the crowds and the lights. There was no way the previous night could be reproduced tonight. "You've got a great show, and we'll have great food." She grabbed the handle and opened the door. "Trust me, you'll love it."

She got out, avoiding the stream of people heading down the sidewalks to the marina entrance, but she couldn't avoid Nick as he came around the rear of the car and took her arm. "Okay, this is your show. Lead the way, Doctor."

She nodded, then headed for the gates, trying to ignore his touch on her. The milling crowds that should have been a buffer for her didn't dispel the feeling of him touching her, and she eased away from him on the pretext of turning to look around. Thankfully he let her go, then she glanced at him. "The show's over there," she said, pointing to the main area that funneled out into the ocean. "The boats all get decorated, then they put together a parade of ships. And there's fireworks. It's just wonderful."

"And the food?" he asked.

"In a bit." She motioned to an area near the docking spots. "Over there. We can get a good seat for the show."

"Lead the way," he said. "It's your show."

Exactly, she thought, but just nodded and led the way through the crowd. They had put up benches on the higher dock, and she took Nick up there, but just as she was ready to step up to the last row, Nick caught her by her arm again. She stopped and turned to him, her breath suspended in her chest for a moment.

"This isn't what I had in mind for tonight, but since we're here, why don't we do this right?"

She didn't understand. "What?"

Then he nodded above them, and when she looked up at the archway, she knew she'd been neatly trapped without even foreseeing it. A garland of mistletoe was strung along the archway, directly over them. Then she was looking into Nick's deep blue eyes, and she knew she didn't have a choice. And her last thought before he framed her face with his hands was, this is a safe place, lots of people, no privacy. Safe.

But as he slowly stroked her cheeks with his thumbs, then smiled that smile and whispered, "There's a lot to be said about tradition," Genna knew that nothing she did with this man was safe.

Not when his mouth found hers, when his tongue

gently pressed to her lips, not when she knew she couldn't stop it. When she didn't want to stop it. Her lips parted of their own accord, and her arms lifted to circle his neck, and in a flash of memory from her dream, she knew she'd done this before. In the shadows of his bedroom, with him in the bed with her, and she knew that whatever Nicholas Marsden really was, she wanted this moment to last forever.

She was moving closer, feeling his body against hers, the fit between them so perfect it was as if they'd been made for each other's embrace. As fireworks started to go off, as the parade of lights started, Genna gave in to every impulse in her.

She clung to Nick, giving as well as she took, and she let the sensations that bombarded her filter into her. For a brief moment she had the oddest feeling that with each mingled breath Nick was touching her soul.

8

Nick totally forgot where he was until the fireworks started to go off. And for a moment in time he almost thought the fireworks came from the kiss, not because of the celebration around them. Fanciful and illogical. Traits so foreign to him that it took a minute for him to sort through them. And as he sorted through them, he knew that kissing Genna did set off fireworks in him. Not the kind anyone could see looking at him, but fireworks deep inside that rocked his world.

As he eased her back a bit, he looked down into her face just as a shower of fireworks exploded overhead. Red-and-green light played over her features, exposing her softly parted lips and the way her eyes were almost closed. Oh, yes, she rocked his world. People pushed around them getting to their seats for the parade, and he knew he had to let her go. But it wasn't easy. As a compromise he slipped his arm around her shoulders and held her to his side as they went silently into the viewing area.

Neither one spoke as they found seats on the benches and turned to the boats that started parallel to the shore, lights draping from their masts and outlining their hulls. Nick watched them, but he never forgot the woman at his side, the woman who let him keep his arm around her, and the woman who seemed to block out everything else.

When he heard the ringing of his cell phone, it jarred him, then he eased away from her and reached in the pocket of his jacket for his phone. He flipped it open and answered it. "Yes?"

"He wants another meeting before the party tomorrow evening. What do you want me to do?" Eileen asked.

Nick looked at Genna, who was watching the parade. "Tell him he'll have an hour tomorrow afternoon at one. That's it."

"Okay."

"Eileen? Tell him that's it. If he doesn't straighten this out tomorrow, tell him there won't be another meeting."

"I'll call him right back."

Nick flipped the phone shut and put it back in his pocket right when Genna turned to look at him. "Will there be another meeting if he doesn't do what you want?"

That took him aback. He hadn't even thought she was listening to his call, much less understanding what he was telling Eileen. "No there won't be. That's my bottom line."

"Are you bluffing?"

"No. Why?"

She shrugged, a fluttery movement of her slender shoulders. "Do you always get what you want?"

A huge yacht came into view then, done all in red lights from stem to stern, and the strains of Christmas music started over loudspeakers, making any talk impossible. He looked at Genna, at the way her jaw was tilted up slightly and her eyes narrowed by her long lashes, hiding the expression he knew was there.

If he got what he wanted, he wouldn't be here right now. Not in a crowd at all. He'd be somewhere alone with Genna, just loving her. That thought jarred him to the core. Loving her. Making love to her, he amended, but it didn't quite feel right. Love. He blinked, trying to clear his thought process, but nothing cleared it when she was inches from him. He could reach out and touch her. Just one simple movement and she'd be in his arms.

But he couldn't do it. Not here. Not now. Not when he could feel something pushed between them, something he didn't understand. But he realized that he'd take his time finding out what it was and getting rid of it. Another first for him. He'd never worked at a relationship in his life, until he knew that this was one worth working for.

"Who ever gets what they want?" he murmured as he leaned closer to her.

"I think you do," she said. "But I've got the feeling, once you get it, you lose interest and move on."

He drew back from a truth that had been an absolute until just moments ago. "I thought you weren't going to analyze me anymore."

"I'm sorry. It's habit," she said as the parade ended. She looked away, then stood as the seats began to empty and people headed for the exit.

Genna stared out at the boats as they headed southward, fighting the taste of Nick in her mouth and the feeling that all she had to do would be to shift a fraction of an inch for his thigh to press against hers. She was very still, wishing she could block out the idea that when Nick got what he wanted, he walked away from it. The game was over. The conquest complete. There was nothing else there for him after that. In business or in his personal life.

She knew that type. She studied them in her work, but she'd never had to deal with a man like that in her personal life. A man like Nick. She swallowed bitterness that burned her tongue. Then as she felt Nick shift and turn, she did the same. And immediately another round of fireworks exploded into the heavens.

Genna shivered slightly at the sight, reliving the

moment they'd first gone off when Nick had kissed her. It startled her when Nick leaned close to her and asked, "Are you cold?"

She was. She'd been cold since Nick had let her go after the kiss, but she shook her head. "No, but it's time to go."

"What about our food?"

She glanced at him, shielding the full image of him by lowering her lashes a bit. "Food. Sure," she murmured, and moved away from him. But he was by her, walking with her, and as they went through the gates of the marina, she motioned away from where he'd parked his car. "It's just down this way," she said. "We can walk." And they wouldn't be shut up in that small car together.

They walked along the sidewalk, past closed stores with their Christmas windows: surf boards draped with pine boughs and brief swimming suits decorated with red and green bows. She hadn't had any place in particular in mind when they'd started walking, just to keep moving and stay out of close places with Nick. Then she spotted a small Mexican restaurant near the boardwalk and headed for it.

Nick didn't say a thing as she pushed back a wrought-iron gate in a low adobe wall and walked into the tiled courtyard. There was just a scattering of diners in the restaurant itself when they went inside, and they were quickly seated in a booth near the windows that looked out onto the beach.

She glanced across the table at Nick as he settled in the chair opposite her and knew that just because there wasn't a grand piano playing softly in the background, and elegant surroundings, that didn't mean his effect on her was lessened. In this tiny, cramped place with recorded Mexican music, mismatched chairs and an imitation Christmas tree, Nick still carried an impact that was hard for her to absorb.

"You said you're hungry, and the food here is good," she said.

Nick looked around, then back at her. "You've been here before?"

"A lot of times," she said.

"So, you stay around here when you're in town?"

She hadn't realized how her own words were trapping her until Nick asked her that, and she backpedaled a bit. "I've been by here. Who hasn't been to the pier?"

"Me."

She frowned at him. "You've never been down here before?" Then she shook her head before he could answer. "No, of course you haven't. This isn't your taste, is it?"

"I don't know. I told you I've never been here before."

"If you want to go someplace else, we can—"

"No, this is great." He picked up a menu a waitress placed in front of them, then flipped the plastic folder open. "Besides, I'm starving."

The waitress was there, a dark girl with a big smile for Nick. "Merry Christmas. What can I get for you?"

Nick glanced at Genna. "How about a margarita?"

"No, no," she said quickly. "A diet cola is just fine."

He smiled at that, but didn't comment as he ordered himself a margarita and Genna a diet cola. As the waitress left to get the drinks and the busboy brought chips and salsa for them, Nick sat back in the booth. "Had enough to drink for a while?" he asked with a slight teasing edge to his expression.

"More than enough," she breathed. "I don't usually drink at all." She grimaced at the memory. "You can see why I don't."

"Oh, it wasn't that bad," he murmured. "Someone once said that the fastest way to get to know someone was seeing them drink."

"If that's true, you know that I'm an easy drunk."

"Easy, but you didn't get crazy or angry, and you didn't start crying or giggling uncontrollably." He grinned at her, an expression that took years off his features. A boyish, charming look that was about as endearing as anything Genna had ever seen before. "And you didn't dance on the tables or strip."

The waitress brought the drinks and she took a

sip. "I can't tell you how thankful I am that I didn't dance on the tables or strip."

He didn't drink any of his margarita yet. Instead, he touched the stem of the glass with one finger and kept his blue eyes on her. "What *do* you remember about last night?"

"Not much after the time on the dance floor," she said. "If I was one of my patients I'd tell them to never drink again after something like that."

"Now you're analyzing yourself. You really shouldn't do that."

"Another bad habit," she murmured, and took another sip of the cola. "And an impossibility, actually."

"What's impossible?"

"Analyzing myself." She fingered the coolness on the glass, then reached for a chip and dipped it in the salsa. "No one ever understands themselves, not in this life."

"No self-awareness, no inner revelation?" he asked with that touch of a smile again.

She looked at Nick and knew how wrong she'd just been. An inner revelation was there, stark and very real. If things had been different, very different indeed, Nicholas Marsden was a man she could really care about. And that revelation was the last thing she wanted to understand. Quickly she took a bite of the chip and salsa, and the heat was immediate and fiery.

She gasped, choking on the peppery salsa, and grabbed for her cola. But as she touched the glass, she hit it with her fingertips and sent it reeling over onto the table, splashing the cola everywhere. Nick was on his feet immediately, the drink spotting his suit coat, but he didn't seem to notice. He was reaching for his napkin, pressing it to the tabletop and waving to the waitress with his other hand.

"Miss, some milk right away, please," he called to her.

Genna's eyes watered as her mouth and throat burned and the cola spread over the table top. She coughed, then the woman was there with a glass of milk and she drank it thankfully. Almost immediately the burning started to subside and she put down the empty milk glass, then swiped at her running eyes. "Oh," she gasped. "Wow, that is so hot. I...I..." She reached for her napkin, but it was soaked, too. "What a mess."

"No problem, ma'am," the waitress said as she soaked it up, then cleared the table. When she finally left and Genna was facing Nick again, a Nick with his suit coat gone and his shirt unbuttoned at the throat, she knew that the burn of salsa and the soaking from cola wouldn't change her caring about Nick.

Care about Nick? Oh, God, she could do a lot more than care about the man. She swallowed hard, the burning in her mouth almost gone. "Thanks for the milk," she said, her voice slightly hoarse.

"See how well I'm getting to know you?" he said with a slow, easy smile. "You're an easy drunk, and you can't handle spicy food."

She didn't want him to know her at all. "Spicy food is one thing, but that...that salsa should be used for torture." She coughed softly. "It should have a warning label on it."

So should Nick, she added to herself. Warning, Any Woman Getting Too Close Will Be In Danger Of Losing Any and All Control. Of Falling Under His Spell. But no warning would do any good for her.

The waitress came back then with fresh drinks, chips and another dish of salsa. "Our mild salsa," she said, as she stood back. "Are you ready to order?"

Nick looked at Genna. "Do you know what you want?"

Dammit all, why did the single word *you* spring into her mind. A bare fact. A painful fact. She wanted Nick. She'd been so sure Belinda had been foolish and easy. But she wasn't any better. Maybe even worse. She should know a lot better. "The number six," she said, not even caring what a number six was. She just wanted this over with.

Nick ordered for himself, then looked at her again

as the waitress left. "After the salsa, I didn't think you'd order something like that."

"Excuse me?"

"The burrito verde. Isn't that hot?"

Very hot. "If I'm prepared, I can handle it," she said.

"Let's hope so." He took a drink of his fresh margarita, then asked her, "You came down here for Christmas?"

"Yes."

"What are you doing Christmas Eve?"

"Excuse me?"

"Christmas Eve. Do you have anything planned for it?"

"Why?"

"Why not?" he asked, and she had the oddest feeling that the question was very important to him.

"I meant, why do you want to know?"

He fingered his glass, and the blue eyes pinned her. "My family has a party every year. The one I told you about. It's a tradition." He paused at those words, and she heard them echoing from when they'd stood under the mistletoe, *a tradition*. "I was wondering if you'd come with me?"

She didn't want to get involved with his family. That was the last thing she wanted. This was between him and her and Belinda. Not his parents. Besides, by Christmas Eve this would all be over and Belinda would be back. "A family get-together to make contacts? I remember."

"It's a ball. I mean, a real ball, with about two hundred guests, mostly business associates."

"I don't think I'd fit in a place like that."

"That's just why I'd like you to come." He sat forward with his forearms on the table. "Every year I dread it. I go, I mingle, I say the right things, make the right contacts, but I never enjoy it. It's no party for me. It never has been. I actually never expected it to be." He studied her for a long moment. "I've got a feeling if you're there, I'll enjoy it."

He almost looked sincere, and maybe a bit lonely for a moment. No, she wouldn't let him do this to her. Emotional blackmail. She was actually feeling sorry for him. Poor little rich boy, who had no fun. It would have been laughable if he hadn't seemed so sincere. "I don't think it would be a good idea," she said. "Besides, I've got plans."

"Plans?"

"A friend and I already made plans." She took a quick drink of the soda, then put the glass back on the table. When she looked at Nick, she found him just staring at her. She could feel her nerves bunching, and she finally said, "What?"

"Change your plans."

Genna wished she could step back and take an easy breath, something she hadn't done since meeting Nick. But she knew she didn't have the luxury of protecting herself that way. "I don't think I can." If anything came easily to Nick, she knew he'd lose interest in her, and she didn't want him to, not just yet. "It's not that easy."

"It's possible?"

"Maybe."

"What about getting together on Christmas Day?"

"Do you have a big family gala then, too?"

"Actually, no. Just me and my family, and the staff of cooks who make the meal."

"Why don't we just do what we're doing now and worry about tomorrow tomorrow?"

"Live for the moment?"

"Why not? What else is there?"

He nodded. "You've got a point. And I can do that."

"I know you can."

He studied her intently. "How do you know that?"

Because you didn't hesitate doing it with Belinda, she thought, but murmured as a substitute, "Your apartment."

He frowned. "What?"

"It's not even furnished. It's almost bare."

"And what is that supposed to mean, Doctor?"

She studied him from under her lashes. "You're asking me to analyze something? I thought you hated that."

"I'm asking this time. Go ahead."

She took a slightly shaky breath. "On general terms, it probably points to a person who doesn't like to make commitments, who has his focus on other things, more important things. Maybe a person who doesn't like to settle down, to lay down roots, or a person who fights against any restraints. A person who lives for the moment."

"You make me sound like some sort of party animal, moving through life, living for the moment, shrugging off any consequences." His eyes narrowed on her, and a frown tugged between his eyes. "Is that what you're saying?"

"I'm just guessing."

"What about if it shows a person who just moved in and hasn't had time to furnish the place because he's been too busy to even call a decorator to come in and see it?"

She knew her face was getting red and hated it. "I told you, I was guessing."

He took a drink of his margarita, then studied her intently. "Now the question is, when do I get a chance to analyze your place?"

The thought of him being in her apartment in San Francisco was oddly unsettling. "I'd show you, but it's clear up in San Francisco," she said, trying to keep her voice light and teasing. "So, that's out."

"Why?"

"In case you forgot, San Francisco is about five hundred miles north of here."

He sipped more of his drink, then put it down and cast her a shadowed look. "Let's fly up there now. Let's live for the moment."

"It's the holidays. There's no way you could get a seat on any plane flying out to San Francisco, even if you wanted to."

"Who said anything about reservations? I've got the company jet. We can get to the airport in…" He glanced at his Rolex, then back at her. "In less than an hour we can be in the air." His blue eyes narrowed with intensity. "So, how about it? Ready to live for the moment?"

"You're kidding," she breathed.

"Do I look like I'm kidding?" he asked, and that smile came—a slow, easy smile that took her breath away.

9

Nick hadn't been kidding.

In less than an hour, true to his word, they were in a private jet that belonged to Marsden Industries, high above the California coast, sitting opposite each other in a cabin that looked almost like a comfortable den.

Genna sat in a high-backed chair that swiveled to take advantage of the night view out the windows, or to face Nick, who was in a similar chair across a small table fixed to the plush carpet-covered floor. Just after takeoff, she was facing Nick and wondering just how crazy she really was.

He was sitting back in his chair, cradling a drink he'd produced from a small refrigerator near the chairs, and he was studying Genna. "Don't tell me you're a white-knuckles flier?"

"Me? No, I'm not."

He glanced at her hands, clutching the plush arms of the chair. "Then why the death grip on the chair?"

She eased her fingers on the leather and forced herself to sink back in the luxury of the chair. "I was just thinking this is crazy."

"I think it's only fair," he murmured.

"Fair?"

"You saw my place, and now I get to see yours."

"But this has to cost a fortune to fly up there on a whim."

"Are you sure you won't have a drink?"

"No, thanks," she said, intent on not having a repeat of the night before. This time she wouldn't be drunk, and she'd stay in control. But she didn't know how she could sit across from Nick like this for an hour. The man drew her like a moth to a flame, and she tempered that with the knowledge that he drew many women in the same way, especially Belinda. That last thought made her stomach hurt, and she fumbled with her seat belt and murmured, "The rest room?"

He motioned behind him with his head. "Right by the door to the cockpit. On the right."

"Thanks," she said, and stood, anxious to get some distance from Nick. But as she moved to pass Nick in the chair, the bottom seemed to drop out of the world. The whole plane lunged downward. She reached for support, then found it with Nick as she fell sideways on top of him.

The next thing she knew, she was sitting in his lap, his arms around her as a voice came over a hidden speaker. "Sorry, Mr. Marsden. Didn't see that coming. Everything okay back there?"

Blue eyes were on her, never looking away as Nick circled her with his arm. "Okay," he called without looking away from Genna. "Probably an air pocket," he murmured to her.

"An air pocket," she repeated in a whisper, knowing she should get up and get out of there, but unable to do even the simplest thing at that moment.

"They happen," he said, one hand resting on her hip, the other around her back.

"Sure," she breathed, fascinated by the gold that flecked the blue of his eyes. Like the flashes of brilliance from the fireworks earlier. And heat, his heat, everywhere, almost fire where his hands touched her, where her body was pressed to his. Fire. Fire that was flickering inside her, surging through her.

Then his hand on her hip moved, feathering up along her arm to cup her neck warmly and gently urging her down toward him. She knew she should fight it, that she should get out of there, but as his lips came closer to hers, she had no fight in her.

His lips found hers, the contact less substantial than a feather brushing her mouth, but so riveting that the rest of the world might not exist. She didn't hesitate in lifting her arms to circle his neck, and that act of surrender was all Nick seemed to need. The caress deepened into an explosion of need and emotions that were raw and pulsating.

His lips and tongue ravished her, and she gave as well as got. The need for this man in her was stunning, demanding more and more, and she held on to him as if he was her lifeline in a sea of insanity. She wanted to be closer than she could be, molding herself to him, straining against him, and his lips burned into hers. His hands shifted, one tugging at her top, finding its way under the soft wool to touch her bare skin.

She gasped as heat found heat, and her gasps turned into low moans when his touch on her moved up until it was at her breast. An ache in her was growing, a knotting surge of feeling that almost made her whimper when his fingers found her nipple through the thin lace of her bra. Feelings that were totally new and unique robbed her of her breath, sent her heart hammering against her ribs. Sensations at the core of her being made her whole body feel as if it were alive for the first time in what seemed forever.

She needed to feel Nick, to make skin-to-skin contact, and frantically she tugged at his shirt until the fine linen was gone and she could feel his skin under her palms. Muscle and tension, slick heat, a trembling in him that echoed in her, and she was lost. The need in her for this man overrode everything, every moment of caution and sanity that had been there before.

When she felt him twist in the chair, when she

felt the hard strength of his desire pressing against her, heard him groan in her ear, she knew that she'd never wanted a man as much as she wanted him. She knew that the hands that touched her, touched her in a way no other hands had ever touched her, that the lips that kissed her, that spread fire on her skin everyplace they touched, kissed her in a way no other lips had ever kissed her. And this man. God help her, but this man was a man like no other man she'd ever known in her life.

Someway her sweater was gone, tossed to one side, the bra lace pulled aside, and when Nick found her nipple with his mouth she almost cried out at the shards of pleasure that surged through her. Nothing mattered, nothing but this, and she gave in to the feelings. She arched back, exposing herself to more and more. Needing more and more. And as his fingers slipped into the waistband of her pants, as the button gave way and the zipper undid, she held her breath.

Then his hands slipped under the elastic of her panties, his fingers splaying on her abdomen. The contact only intensified everything, bringing the ache in her to a crescendo that knew no bounds. Then the touch was lower, and as he found her, she sobbed softly, curling toward him as her legs parted. His fingers found her center, his mere touch sending off small explosions in her, the whimpers that she heard, her own.

She pressed toward him, toward the pleasure that his touch was giving her, then he entered her and she gasped. His lips buried in her exposed neck, the feelings almost painfully exquisite, and tears were so very close to the surface. His hand moved in her and over her, and a pleasure almost beyond bearing grew higher and higher. Her hips began to move, matching his rhythm, and just when she felt as if she were going to explode into a million shimmering centers of pleasure, it was gone.

The world fell, lurching downward, sending her plummeting with it, and reality came back with a jarring, horrible, reeling sensation. Nick was gone from her, shifting, holding her back, the contact all but broken. As she opened her eyes, he was there, lifting her up, and she didn't understand until that voice was there again.

"Mr. Marsden, we've got trouble. Thought it was just a fluke, but we've got trouble."

Nick stared at Genna, his eyes as filled with need as she knew hers were. Then he was lifting her back, her feet were on the floor, and he was standing by her. His touch steadied her as he breathed in a rough, hoarse voice, "I'll be back." With a quick, hard kiss, he was letting her go, then he was going toward the front of the plane, and she saw him go through the cockpit door.

Voices were there, talking urgently, but it was all Genna could do to find her sweater and pull it back on over her tender breasts. With unsteady fingers she fastened her pants, then all but dropped back into the chair. The plane was in trouble, but a part of her knew she'd almost fallen into even worse trouble than plane problems. God, she'd let herself go. She'd forgotten about revenge or anger and had fallen into a place that was beginning to terrify her.

She licked her cold lips, the taste of Nick still there, and her body began to tighten again. She took a deep, unsteady breath, then did it again and again until she felt the world begin to settle for her. The voices in the cockpit were a low drone, and as she brushed at her hair to tuck it behind her ears, she felt herself begin to regain some semblance of sanity. Some control. A control that had almost evaporated moments ago.

By the time Nick came back into the cabin, she'd found a degree of composure, a composure that was definitely challenged by the sight of him. Just seeing the way his hair was mussed, his shirt tucked back in yet slightly askew, threatened that composure. But all she had to do was remember Belinda, think about her being touched like that by Nick, falling under his spell like she almost had, and it gave her a degree of protection.

He eyed her as he stopped in front of her, and she braced herself, certain he was going to touch her again. Thankfully he didn't. He moved back and took the chair, but he didn't sit back. He leaned forward, his elbows on his knees and his eyes on her. "Sorry about that interruption," he murmured. "But we've got a problem."

She was surprised that he thought about it that way, until she realized he was talking about the plane, not the two of them. "Oh, the plane? Is it okay?"

"The pilot says there's a problem with the fuel line, and we need to go back to get it corrected." He spread his hands, palms up. "We'll lose an hour or so while he fixes it. Then we can head back on up the coast."

A reprieve, and she grasped at it with both hands. "No, it's late. I need to get back. I've been gone too long as it is."

He hesitated, then nodded. "Sure." He studied her so intently she could feel that knot deep inside her coming back, and she shifted in the seat to try and ease it...or stop it. "Things haven't worked out the way I thought they would," he murmured.

Amen to that, she almost said, but bit her lip. "I...I never expected to be in this plane," she whispered as she made herself sit back and not clasp her hands tightly in her lap. "We can get back okay, can't we?"

"The pilot said there won't be a problem landing again," he said, easing back in the chair and slipping down to stretch his legs out and to loosely lace his fingers together on his stomach. "And we can do this again."

She kept silent, looking down at her hands and wishing they were back at the airport and out of the plane. The feelings that had bombarded her moments ago hadn't died, and try as she would, her body couldn't quite settle. She felt edgy and vaguely frustrated. No, not vaguely. Very frustrated, both physically and with herself for letting it happen at all.

She could barely meet his gaze, but she forced herself to do that very thing. Nick was settled back in his chair, his head resting on the plush leather back and his eyes half-closed. None of the tension in her seemed to be in him, and she resented that. Could he do what he'd just done, get in that deep, then just cut it off? Stupid question, she thought. The man obviously could cut off all and any emotion whenever he decided to.

She swallowed hard, bitterness mingling with the lingering taste of Nick there. "How long will it be before we land?" she asked.

Before Nick could answer, the pilot came over the hidden speakers. "Ten minutes, Mr. Marsden. Fasten the seat belts."

He and Genna did up their belts, and neither of them spoke again until the plane landed and came to a stop by the private hangar in the huge airport. Nick undid his belt, then got up without a word and went into the cockpit again. Genna got free of the belt, then stood, and by that time Nick was back in the cabin.

He nodded to her. "Okay, let's get out of here," he said. He came toward her, his hand out, and she moved quickly, turning away from him and heading for the door.

She hurried down the metal steps on the side of the sleek jet and stepped down onto the tarmac into the chill of the December evening. The roar of jets overhead made talking impossible, and Genna walked with Nick by her side to the hangar where his Porsche was parked.

By the time they got out of the airport area and headed back toward the city, Genna knew she needed space, a break from being near Nick. She had to regroup and steel herself for the end of this. She almost jumped out of her skin when Nick spoke as they hit the Coast Highway.

"Where are you staying?"

"Excuse me?" she asked, not turning to him, but keeping her gaze on the deep night outside.

"Your address. What is it?"

"Why do you need that?"

"To take you home," he said with obvious patience.

She hadn't thought about that at all. "Oh, you can just drop me by the pier and I'll—"

"It's after midnight, and there's no way I'm just

dropping you off at the pier. Now, what's the address?"

He couldn't take her back to Belinda's. Then he'd know everything, and all of this would have been for nothing. Nothing would be solved, and nothing would be settled. So she lied. "I can't go back to the place I'm staying."

"Why not?"

"It's late and I don't have a key. I don't want to wake up everyone by dragging in this late. I...I thought I'd just get a hotel room for the night."

"That's another problem. How many hotels do you think will have space over the holidays?"

He was right again, and she hated it. "I-I'll call around. I'm sure I can find something."

He reached in his pocket and took out his cell phone. "Be my guest," he said.

She took the phone, not missing the way the warmth of his body was still caught in the plastic. She stared down at it. "I don't suppose you have a phone book?"

"Sorry. No phone book."

She handed the phone back to him. "Just stop by a phone booth, and I'll see if I can get the number of some hotels nearby."

He drove south toward Santa Monica and said, "I've got a better idea."

For a moment she was sure he was going to suggest that they go back to his place. "What idea?" she asked, not at all sure she wanted to know.

"The company keeps a place at the Richman Towers. That's not too far from here, and it's empty."

"What sort of place?"

"A corporate suite. The place you put out-of-town clients and associates when they come in for business. No one's using it. It's yours if you want it."

"No, I couldn't, I mean, I—"

He downshifted. "It's there. It's not being used. It's yours for the night, or I can take you to a phone booth, call around and find a room someplace else."

It sounded stupid to insist on the latter route, and accepting his offer kept their contact alive but in a safe way. "Okay, for one night. I'd appreciate it."

After all, it wasn't his place. It was an impersonal hotel room. An empty hotel room. She knew that Nick looked at her for a long moment, but she didn't turn as he said, "Fine." And the car sped up.

The Richman Towers was a place that looked as unlike a hotel as any place she'd ever seen. It rose into the night sky off one of the main streets in Bel Air: a glass and stone structure at least twenty stories high and framed at the front by a stone portico and green awnings. A discreet brass sign hung by the door, and a green-uniformed doorman, who stood by the glass entrance, nodded to the two of them as they went into the vast lobby.

The place was beyond classy, into the high-rent district of overt opulence, with marble and gilt everywhere. Nick nodded to the man on duty behind the registration desk, but kept going to the elevators. Passing the bank of brass doors framed by potted plants, he led Genna to a single door with just a slot for a card in the wall beside it.

Nick took out a card, slipped it in the slot, and the door opened silently. He let Genna go in ahead of him, then the door closed behind them, and in a matter of seconds they were on the twentieth floor, stepping out into a small reception hallway that had two doors opening off it. Nick motioned to the door on the left.

Genna went to the door with him, then turned to Nick. "Thanks for this," she said.

He stood very close, so close she could feel each breath he took, but he didn't move to go inside with her. He handed her the card, and as she closed her fingers around it, he moved toward her, touched his lips to hers, but drew back almost before the caress began. With a crooked smile he whispered, "Sleep well." Then he turned and crossed back to the elevator door. "I'll call here in the morning."

She turned from him, thankful to have a breather before she had to end this whole charade. She slid the card into the slot by the door despite the way her hand was shaking, then as the lock clicked softly and the door silently swung open, she glanced back at Nick. He was watching her with a smile, and as their eyes met, his smile faltered.

For a moment they just looked at each other, then he touched his fingertips to his lips and turned from her to reach for the button for the elevator. She slipped into the dark hotel room, closed the door behind her and finally was able to take a full breath into her lungs.

All she could make out inside was what was exposed from the city glow that filtered in through partially draped windows on the far side of the space. She went toward the view without turning on the lights, her feet sinking into deep, plush carpeting. Silently she crossed the shadowy room, and just before she got to the windows, she knew she wasn't alone.

At the same time she heard someone breathing heavily, she collided with something, her foot striking a soft mass. A gasp echoed in the space, then Genna screamed as a hand reached out and grabbed her leg, sending her pitching forward into the darkness.

10

Nick was congratulating himself on his control for kissing Genna and then walking away, when he heard the scream. He was back at the door to the suite before he realized he'd run there. But he was faced by the closed door. He'd given the card to Genna.

Just when he called out, "Genna? What's going on?" the door flew open and he was faced with a man, no a boy, probably a teenager, half-dressed in the uniform of the staff in the hotel. The boy was disheveled, his jacket clutched in one hand, his shirt open, and his other hand grabbing the waistband of his pants that had the fly undone.

Right behind him was a terrified looking girl whose lipstick was all over the boy's face. "Oh, man, I'm sorry," the boy was muttering as Nick moved into the suite. He reached for the light, and the glare exposed even more. The boy's frightened and embarrassed look, the girl's confusion and anger, and then he turned and saw Genna.

She was sitting on the floor braced in a sitting position with her hands pressed to the plush beige carpeting, her eyes wide with shock.

"Man, hey, I'm so sorry," the boy was stammering. "Please, I'm out of here. I thought the place was empty, and Carol wanted to see it, and things just...I didn't mean to scare anyone."

Nick looked back at the boy, then down at the name stitched on his rumpled shirt. "Ralph," he said. "Get yourself and the girlfriend out of here...now."

"I'm real sorry, man, real sorry. My boss, he's going to kill me." He did up his pants as he babbled on and on. "Is there any way you'd just let this go? Me and Carol, we'll do anything. I swear."

Nick shook his head. "Just get out and we'll forget all about it."

"Oh, man, thanks," Ralph said, and hesitated as if he was going to shake hands with Nick, then he thought better of it. Instead, he grabbed the girl's hand and said, "I owe you, man, I owe you." Then he pulled the girl out through the door with him. "We're going, but if you need anything while you're here, just ask for Ralph, and I'll be up here so fast it'll make your head swim. Anything you want, you've got it. And if you—"

Nick cut off his words by reaching for the door and swinging it shut with a loud thud. Then he turned and crossed to where Genna was still sitting splay-legged on the carpet looking up at him. "Teenage hormones," he murmured.

"I thought it was a body or something at first," she said, then he saw a glimmer of humor in her eyes. "A body. I tripped over it. I was scared to death, then I heard this voice saying, 'Man, we're dead,' and the body was moving."

"Oh, Ralph and his girlfriend are very alive," he said as he reached out his hand to help her to her feet.

Her fingers closed around his, slender and warm, and as he pulled her effortlessly to her feet, he found himself smiling as she started to smile. "Very alive," she whispered. "And full of life." She started to laugh. "Very full of life."

Still holding her hand in his, Nick heard Genna give a perfect impression of poor Ralph. "I owe you, man, I owe you. If you need anything while you're here, just ask for Ralph, and I'll be up here so fast it'll make your head swim. Anything you want, you've got it."

By the time she finished, he was laughing out loud and wondered if he'd ever felt like this. So free to laugh. Not that polite stuff he did when a client thought he'd said something amusing, or when Mars told one of his awful "knock-knock" jokes, but a laughter that came from deep in his being. "You've got Ralphy boy down perfectly."

"He was easy, so was that poor girl, obviously,"

Genna said around her own laughter. "When the lights went on she looked scared to death."

"He probably told her that he had the right to this place." This humor was fascinating to him, a thread of it going on and on with each word she uttered. "Acting like a big man, then getting caught with his pants down. Teenage lust in the penthouse."

"That sounds like a really bad B movie," she said.

"I Was A Teenage Stud," Nick countered.

That brought fresh laughter from Genna, but her hand stayed in his as she pressed her other hand to her middle. "Oh, boy, yes, you've got it," she gasped. "Mr. Studly in a uniform."

"Mr. Studly?" he asked.

"Mr. Studly and his studette?"

Their mixed laughter seemed to surround Nick, as seductive in its way as anything had been in his life. But the laughter began to falter as he looked into those dark eyes and saw an echo of his own feelings there. His hand holding hers was their only contact, yet somehow Nick felt more joined to Genna in that moment than he had since they first met. Even more so than those moments on the plane. And it confused him at the same time it excited him.

Her laughter faltered, too, and he knew she was feeling it, too, that the sensations in him seemed to be reverberating in her. And the humor was gone. As suddenly as it had come, it was gone, and in its wake was a need so desperate in him to hold her, that it shook him.

Slowly he drew her to him, and as she came to him, the feelings on the plane were pale in comparison. When his mouth found hers, he knew he'd been waiting for this moment since the first time he saw Genna. Or maybe from the beginning of his life. He didn't know which.

All he knew was he was right where he wanted to be, where he'd probably wanted to be forever, but just hadn't known it. He tasted her, relishing her essence in his mouth, and feeling her press to him. Her breasts crushed against his chest, her hips pressing to his, and her mouth opened to him in invitation. The laughter was gone, but not the seductive power this woman had, just being here. A seductive power that literally stunned him.

Genna didn't know when the laughter changed to need, or when it had stopped being a strangely shared joke about Ralph and his girlfriend and turned into a seduction that came out of nowhere. She didn't care. She didn't care about anything right then except feeling Nick against her, having his hands on her, his lips draining her of all reason and strength to fight what was happening.

She never turned back. She knew, somewhere from the fringes of her sanity, that she should be running like mad. That this was the time to pull out, to let him fall flat on his face and get the hell out of here, but she couldn't. There was nothing in her to stop this. There was nothing in her to grasp at sanity of any sort. And when his hands worked their way under her sweater, she relished the feeling of skin on skin. His touch was gentle, yet exploring, and before she knew it her sweater was gone, tossed to one side.

For a brief moment Nick stood there just looking at her, his gaze potent as it trailed from her lips to her breasts, barely covered by her bra. She could feel strings being pulled in her, feelings coming from a place she never knew existed, her nipples hardening in anticipation. She wanted Nick. She wanted him more than life itself right then. And she could tell he wanted her just as desperately.

His jacket was gone, tossed over to where her sweater rested on the carpet. Then she reached out, and with unsteady fingers slowly undid the buttons on his shirt. As the fine linen opened, she saw his chest with a light sprinkling of dark hair, the hard muscles of his stomach, and she eased the shirt back and off his shoulders. She wanted a skin-on-skin contact, to feel his heat and his strength.

With a low moan she dipped her head and touched her lips to his chest. She felt his breath catch in him and a faint unsteadiness in his muscles, then he tangled his fingers in her hair, gently tugging her head back until she was looking into his blue eyes. The fire in her was there in the depths of his gaze, and no words were necessary. No words came between them. As his other hand touched her back, then undid her bra, she accepted the action. She wanted it. She shrugged off the light lace of her bra, letting the straps slide down her arms, then she flicked it away from them.

When Nick reached for her again, she knew that there was no stopping any of this. She was committed, and any thought of bringing it to a halt had been cast aside by a need in her that was akin to a physical hunger for this man. When he lifted her into his arms, cradling her to his chest, she put her arms around his neck. A flashing memory came to her of the other night when she'd been drunk. He'd held her like this, she knew that now. He'd carried her like this. But tonight was as different from that night as black was from white.

Tonight she wasn't drunk. She couldn't use that excuse. And tonight she wanted him. She wanted to be held by him, to be touched by him, to be possessed by him. As he carried her into a shadowy room, she pressed her lips to his shoulder and felt him jerk with a response. Then they were at a huge bed, and they fell together into the coolness of the linen.

Nick was by her, his hands exploring her, touching her in spots that drew soft moans from her. She arched to his strokes, biting her lip at the intensity of the feelings that his fingers were building in her.

His hands found her breasts, tracing the hardening nipples, then his lips took his hand's place, while he trailed his fingers down her stomach to the fastener on her pants.

Awkwardly she tried to help him with the button, then pushed at her pants until they were tangled around her legs and he tugged the fabric free of her legs. Her hands found the buckle of his belt, shaking so badly that she could barely undo the buckle, then tug the leather free of his pants. When she reached for his waistband, he moved back and away from her.

When she almost cried out from the loss of his touch and the feeling of his body by hers, she realized he was standing by the bed. He was stepping out of his pants, then quickly took off white Jockey shorts. In the softness of the shadows she could see his desire, his need as great as hers, then he was back with her. He rolled onto the linen, his touch sending fire through her veins, then his fingers slipped under the elastic of her panties.

It was a repeat of what had happened on the airplane, his touch going lower and lower until he found the center of her being. She cried out at the contact, then the flimsy nylon of her panties was gone, and she was naked before him, yearning toward the pressure of his hand on her. She never knew that anything could feel that overwhelmingly pleasurable, almost painful in its intensity.

Then she found out that those feelings were only the beginning. He explored her with his fingers, pressing the heel of his hand against her and slowly making seductive circles with his hand. The feelings grew and grew, threatening to explode in a frenzy of pure pleasure. Just when she thought she'd die from the ecstasy surrounding and running through her, she was pulled back from the brink.

Nick was over her, bracing himself with his hands on either side of her shoulders, and in the shadows she looked up at him. One word came to her, a word that threatened to destroy her. *Love.* She loved him. And in that moment of total lucidity, she made a decision that she knew was wrong, yet the only thing she could do. She reached out to him, lifting her hips to him and inviting him to take her.

For tonight she was lost to the world. She was here with Nick and that was all that mattered. And she'd have him...once...and to hell with the consequences of her actions. She'd deal with those later. Much later. She felt his strength against her, testing her, and she trembled spontaneously, then gasped as he pressed into her, filling her.

For a long moment neither moved, then Nick began to slowly lift his hips, then thrust them back down, and Genna stopped all thinking. She went with the feelings, lifting her hips higher to his thrusts, welcoming them, her fingers pressing into his shoulders, almost afraid that he'd stop. And if he did, she knew she'd die.

But he didn't stop. His thrusts grew faster and deeper, bringing with them feelings that grew and grew inside her. Just when she was certain she couldn't take it anymore, that the line between ecstasy and pain was being blurred, she felt herself being thrown into a realm that was made just for her and Nick. And no one else.

She heard two voices cry out in unison, then she was lost. She fell into brilliance and joy that knew no bounds. And the only thing that kept her anchored to the world was Nick and being joined with him. Her anchor, her joy, and she never looked back.

Nick never looked back, either. He had wanted Genna from the first, and this seemed as natural as breathing to him. And just as important to him as living. He felt her by him, the small shudders as the feelings subsided, and he relished the way she lay against him, one hand resting on his heart.

"Remind me to leave a big tip for Ralph," he breathed as he brushed at the tangled hair around her face.

She moved closer, her cheek pressed to his shoulder. "Why?"

"If it wasn't for him, I would have kept going and left you here alone." His touch on her was unsteady, and he knew that even though she'd satisfied him more than he'd dreamed possible, he still wanted her. And he knew he'd want her over and over and over again.

"Alone?" she echoed in a voice so soft he had to strain to make it out.

"The last thing I wanted tonight was to be alone," he admitted with a truthfulness that shook him. If he'd left here without her, he would have been well and truly alone. And that thought disturbed him.

He slipped his arm around her shoulders, drawing her so close he could feel every inch of her against his nakedness. "The boy's getting a big tip," he murmured, then shuddered faintly when her hand moved on his chest, lightly brushing over his nipple.

"Shhhh," she said softly. "No more talking. Not now."

He took an unsteady breath as he said, "You're right. No more talking." His fingers tangled in her hair, and he simply held her to him, letting the feeling of having her there with him, filter into his soul. Later he'd understand all of this...later. But for now she was here, and in the morning he'd wake to her, see her face, and he wouldn't be alone. That was enough for now.

Genna didn't want to talk, not when she knew in some corner of her mind that not only had she been out-classed by an expert in seduction, but she'd fallen headlong in love with him. And that thought terrified her as it grew more and more solid in her mind.

She didn't want to love him. But even as she denied it to herself, she knew it was too late for denials or pretense. She loved Nick. Plain and simple. No, never simple, but it was a fact. And her heart sank as he slowly stroked his fingers along her bare shoulder. Through the shadows, she looked at his face, at eyes still heavy with fulfillment, eyes watching her, and she knew that the love was irrevocable, as irrevocable as her need for him.

When he lifted his hand and brushed her cheek with the tips of his fingers, she shivered, and when he drew her closer to him, she didn't fight it. She went to him, relishing the way her body fit neatly against his, as if it had been made for this very moment. And when he started caressing her again, running his hands over her, finding her spots where passion exploded with just a mere touch, she knew that the love she had for him was forever. And totally destructive for everyone.

But that didn't stop her from lifting her lips to his, from offering herself to him, and when he spanned her waist with his hands and lifted her easily to sit astride him, she relished every touch, every moment. It was all she'd have, and she wanted it as much as life itself.

As she sank down, as he filled her, she arched back, and even though she knew there was no forgiveness for what she was doing to Belinda and to herself, she plunged headlong into the sensations. She moved with Nick, and for that moment in time, everything else was forgotten but an incredible feeling of being truly one with him.

11

Denial. Genna had talked to patients about it often enough to have the definition down pat. But as she lay awake after Nick had drifted into a heavy sleep, she tried to hide behind denial. She didn't want to leave the space she'd found by Nick. She didn't want to move out of his hold, to feel his hands leave her, to lose his heat by her side or the way he nuzzled his chin into her hair.

She lay very still in the shadows, making herself breathe evenly, wishing it would never stop, but reality became more and more solid all the time. And with that reality came a deep pain that pushed all the pleasure and the joy aside. And in their place came the knowledge that she'd violated every shred of common sense she'd ever possessed.

Common sense? She almost laughed at that, until Nick sighed by her and shifted, his hand slipping off her hip. How could she have let this happen? How could the seducer have been seduced, and how could she love him? That last thought made her stomach lurch and sickness rise in her.

So much for revenge. So much for taking care of Belinda. She cringed at the thought of her friend. What had she done for her? Slept with the man Belinda thought she loved? She knew it was over, that whatever she'd allowed to happen was gone. And she had to leave.

She looked at Nick, sound asleep by her, and wished she could hate him. She wished she could build a wall of anger, but all the anger was at herself. And all the pain was hers. She gently disengaged herself from his touch, feeling deep, horrible isolation when she was free. Then she silently got up and went through the shadows to find her clothes.

She dressed quickly, and without a backward glance, she stole out of the hotel suite and left. As she got into the elevator, she saw her reflection in the mirrors that lined the car, and it shocked her that she looked so much like she had the day before. Nothing on the outside showed the pain she'd inflicted on herself. Or the remorse that welled up inside her, remorse mingled with a sadness that she could only define as a form of grief.

She got out and walked through the predawn lobby, headed for the doors, and with each step she took, she grabbed at anger. Even if it was directed at herself, she didn't care. She clung to it, building a wall against the emptiness that was growing in her.

And by the time she got back to Belinda's apartment, she felt as if she could do what she had to do. Then leave.

Nick woke to an empty room, and he didn't have to turn or reach out beside him to know that his dream of waking up with Genna by him was gone. He pushed himself up, seeing the first rays of sun filtering through the partially curtained windows and felt a loneliness that ate at him. He got up and showered, then dressed and finally stood in the middle of the empty hotel suite.

He wanted to see Genna, to look at her and remember the night before. He wanted to see the reality of what his memories held, but he didn't even know where to start to find her. Yet something in him knew that she'd get in touch with him, and she'd do it at the office. The way she had the day before. He looked at the clock and found it was almost nine o'clock. Eileen would have been there for an hour.

He put in a call to Eileen and got her on the first ring. "Eileen, it's me. Any messages for me?"

"One."

"What is it?"

"Weiss says he's coming by at ten. He's got an offer that his board and ours will back."

That should have made Nick happy, but the only message he wanted was from Genna. "Okay, I'm on my way down there. Get the papers ready and reserve the conference room for ten. And if you get a message from Genna Wade, tell her I'll be there in half an hour, and get a phone number from her where I can reach her. Okay?''

"Will do, boss. Anything else?"

"Any word from Mars?"

"Nary a peep."

"Small mercies," he muttered and hung up.

Genna found a fax on the machine when she walked into Belinda's apartment after the taxi ride home from the hotel. It was a scrawled message that said Belinda was on a flight back and would be there by four that afternoon. The last line said, "Get dressed up. I want your meeting with Mars to be perfect."

As Genna tossed the paper into a wastebasket, she felt her stomach rebel. She wasn't at all certain she could face Belinda, and she knew that facing Nick was out of the question. She couldn't see him again, not ever. But she knew she had to finish what she'd started with Nick.

It took her until that afternoon to finally compose the note she knew she had to send to Nick's office. Draft after draft was torn to pieces before she finally put the last draft into the fax machine. It lay there for a long moment before she could make herself hit the Send button.

As the paper fed through the machine, she turned away from it and headed for the door. She couldn't just stay in here and wait for Belinda to get back. She had to move and feel fresh air on her face. Dressed in old jeans and a well-worn sweatshirt, she went out and headed for the pier area. But with every step she took, the words of her note echoed in her mind.

Nick or Mars, whatever you want to call yourself,
I thought I could do this, get you back at your own game, then walk away with satisfaction that you hurt a fraction of the amount Belinda will be hurting. But I was wrong. I wanted to make this clean and neat, but I was as foolish as Belinda was when she fell for you.

I wanted to say, 'Babe, it's been fun, but it's done,' and leave it at that, but it got out of hand. Nothing I did can change the fact that Belinda is my best friend and I don't want her hurt any more than necessary.

If you have an ounce of decency in you, you'll talk to Belinda face-to-face, you'll meet with her and let her down gently. Ease out of your relationship with her, then get out of her life and leave her alone. Forget anything ever happened and let her start all over again.

Genna.

She headed for the pier, into cold, ocean air and a scattering of people walking by her. The faint strains of Christmas music drifted along the beach, and Genna stopped to face the gray Pacific, where cold sunlight glinted off the choppy waves.

Right then, with memories of Nick washing over her, she felt more alone than she ever had in her life.

And more ashamed than she'd ever felt over any mistake she'd made in her life. She'd been forewarned. She'd known what he was, and she'd thought she could get in and out without him touching her. All of her training did no good. No matter how she looked at it, she felt only shame about whatever it was in her that had let her fall in love with a man like Nicholas Marsden.

Nick was in a second meeting with Weiss, listening to their accountant sort through the financial impact the merger would have on both companies. But instead of listening to figures and projections of profit, Nick was trying to absorb a basic truth. In a life that had been remarkably free of emotional entanglements and centered on cold-blooded business affairs, he'd fallen head over heels in love with Genna.

While the accountant went over charts, Nick savored the fact that he, of all people, could actually love someone. It felt foreign to him, but very right.

By the time he'd agreed to what Weiss wanted from Marsden's, he left the meeting. He told his attorney to take Weiss to the legal department for signatures, then he left them and headed back to his office to wait for Genna to contact him.

As he stepped into the reception area outside his office, he saw Eileen coming out of the com room. When she saw him, she grimaced at him, and it was as if he was replaying the scene from the night she'd brought the fax from the flight attendant to him by the elevator. A lifetime ago. She had a piece of paper caught between her thumb and forefinger and was holding it out in front of her with a frown on her face.

"This for you, I think." She stopped. "Or maybe not."

Nick took the paper, and as he read it, he was confused at first. "Nick or Mars?" It didn't make any sense. "...get you back at your own game..." Game? "Belinda is my best friend and I don't want her hurt." He felt as if he'd been thrown into a place that made no sense. He looked at the signature. "Genna." He reread quickly, trying to make sense out of it. "...Babe, it's been fun, but it's done...an ounce of decency in you...let her down gently...get out of her life...finish this...leave her alone."

He read it a dozen times before he finally began to understand. The meeting at the club hadn't been coincidental. Genna had set it up to try and protect her friend. It had all been a charade, a planned revenge for a friend. Genna thought he was Mars and wanted to get back at him. God, he could barely take it in.

"So, what's this all about?" Eileen asked.

He grimaced at the paper, then shook his head. "A huge mistake," he said. She thought he was Mars, that he'd cut off her friend with a fax. He looked at the number at the top of the fax, and the banner B. Hogan. "Eileen, find out the address for that flight attendant Mars just dropped."

"How can—"

He looked at her. "Knowing Mars, he probably sent her flowers or jewelry on the company account. Look it up, get an address and get it to me as soon as you can."

She frowned at him. "Another crisis with 'regards' from your brother?"

He exhaled. "A crisis, but I'm right in the middle of this one. Just get that address as quickly as you can."

"Hurry, hurry, Eileen," someone said, and Nick turned to see Mars striding into the room.

Mars, the core of all the problems, and Mars, smiling as if he didn't have a care in the world. For the first time since Nick's realization that he would be picking up the pieces for Mars forever, he felt like striking out. One punch to take that smarmy smile off of his brother's face.

"Where in the hell have you been?" Nick snapped.

Mars waved that away with one hand and strode past him heading toward Nick's private office. "Come on inside. I need to talk to you. In private."

"Damned straight you do," Nick muttered, and followed Mars into the office as Eileen left the reception area. The door closed with a bang as Mars dropped down into one of the leather chairs in front of the desk.

Nick circled the desk, not trusting himself to even get close to his younger brother right then. He stared at Mars from behind his marble-topped desk, piled high with unfinished work, work he hadn't been able to concentrate on since meeting Genna. The urge to strangle Mars was pushing out thoughts of hitting him. Strangling him nice and slowly.

Mars, in jeans and a T-shirt with a Harvard logo on it, despite the fact he'd never gone near any university for more than one semester, was oblivious to all the negative energy in the executive office at that moment. He was focused on himself. His usual preoccupation.

"Can we talk?" Mars asked.

"You bet we can."

Mars had the decency to look a bit surprised at the sharp tone Nick used. He knew that this wasn't the usual response he got from Nick. He was used to Nick's exasperation and his annoyance, but not this anger that he finally was noticing. "Nicky, are you all right?"

"Don't call me Nicky," he said harshly. "And, no, I'm not all right."

"Business trouble?" he asked, then waved that aside with the flick of one hand. "No, don't tell me. I wouldn't understand it, anyway. Besides, I've got this problem—"

"You *are* the problem," Nick said. "But you're going to make things better."

His irresponsible, irritating, self-involved and oddly charismatic, kid brother, looked confused for a moment. "What are you talking about? You can't know about my problem. I just realized what had to be done and came back."

"Your problem is Belinda Hogan. Is that name familiar to you at all?"

The shock on his face was genuine. "Belinda? How in the hell did you know—"

"You broke up with her by fax, didn't you?"

Mars sat up and leaned forward, resting his elbows on his knees. He looked oddly uncomfortable, a major step for a man who just didn't give a damn about much of any fallout from his actions. "Nick, what's—"

"Did you or didn't you send that woman a fax to break up with her because you didn't have the guts to face her down and explain why you were taking off and dumping her?"

"Okay, okay, I did. I admit it. I thought it was the best way to do it. She's so...so emotional about things. She thought she was in love with me, and I couldn't take that. It just overwhelmed me."

"You jerk!" Mars flinched as Nick bit out the words. "You incredibly selfish jerk."

"Hey, this doesn't have anything to do with you. Besides, since when have you worried about my girlfriends?"

Nick tried to control his raging anger. "Do you know a woman named Genna Wade?"

"I've never met her, but she's Belinda's best friend, like a sister, from what Belinda told me about her. How do you know about her?"

"Mars, where does the stewardess live?"

"She's a flight attendant, and I—"

"I don't give a damn if she's a brain surgeon! Where does she live?"

"Down by the Santa Monica pier. Why?"

"An address, just give me an address."

He shrugged. "I don't know the address. I just know how to get there."

Nick stood and went around the desk, reaching for Mars and grabbing his arm. "Take me there."

"Nick, you've finally cracked up, haven't you? I told you about working too much, but no, you kept it up." He pulled free of Nick's hold as they got to the door. "You're having a breakdown."

"All I want to break right now is your neck, little brother. Now, tell me how to get there."

Mars flexed his arm, rubbing at where Nick had gripped him. "You don't have to get nasty. I'm going there now. You can come along with me, if you want. Although I can't see what you want to go there for."

That stopped Nick cold. "You're going there? Why? Haven't you done enough damage for one lifetime?"

"That's what I came here to tell you." He grinned, a huge smile from ear to ear. "Nicky, I'm in love. I mean *really* in love. I'm as stunned as you probably are. I thought I could leave and forget about Belinda, but I couldn't. I know you won't understand this, but I'm crazy about her. I can't forget about her. I think about her all the time. I dream about her. I can't eat. I got to Aspen and knew that I had to come back for her. The thing is, the fax I sent. I called her place and there wasn't any answer, so I'm hoping that she's been out of town on a flight and she hasn't seen it yet."

"Don't count on that," Nick muttered, then motioned Mars through the door. "Lead the way to her place."

"Nicky, you don't have to go with me. I'm telling you, I give up. I love her. I'm not going to—"

"Just shut up and take me to her apartment."

Mars looked at Nick, then shrugged. "Whatever," he muttered, and led the way out of the office.

Genna headed back to Belinda's as the sun began to set, and was barely back in the apartment before she heard someone at the door. The next thing she knew, Belinda was there in her flight uniform, smiling hugely at her as she came inside. "Genna," she said with a grin as she dropped her overnight case, crossed the room to Genna and hugged her tightly. "Oh, I'm so glad you're here."

Belinda looked blissfully happy and excited to be back. And Genna could barely control the guilt and the pain that she knew was going to come sooner or later. She tried to smile at her friend and act as casually as she could. "I'm glad you're back," she said as Belinda stood back.

Tall, blond and pretty, Belinda looked sharp in the navy suit she wore for the airlines. "I got here as quickly as I could." She smiled brightly. "I'm so excited about you meeting Mars. You won't believe this man," she said, talking quickly as she stepped out of her low heels and took off her tailored jacket. "He's so great. He's gorgeous and funny and sexy as all get-out." She dropped her jacket on the couch and looked a bit taken aback for a moment. "So, you straightened up? I'll never find anything now."

"Belinda, this Mars, he—"

"He's so great, Genna." She dropped down on the sofa and patted the cushion beside her. "Sit and let's talk. I can't wait for you to meet him."

She could wait forever for that, and with any luck she'd be out of there before "Mr. Perfect" showed up. "You've talked to him today?"

"No, but he knows I'm back. He'll call soon."

As if her words had produced it, the phone rang. She reached for the red lips and answered on the second ring. "Yes?"

One look at the instant smile, and Genna knew who was on the phone. "Mars? I was just talking about you."

She listened, the smile staying in place and joined by a dreamy look in her eyes. "No, no faxes. I just got in. Of course. When?" She sat up. "Now? Where are you?" She stood up. "Wonderful. Of course." Then she hung up and looked at Genna. "He's on his way up. He needs to ask me something."

"Ask you something?" she asked softly.

"Well, he said we needed to talk something over." She stood and hurried across the room to her bedroom. "I need to change. He said he was on his cell phone and almost here, so if he gets here before I'm done, let him in."

"Belinda," Genna said quickly, the idea of answering the door to Nick unbearable. "You look fine. You're beautiful."

Belinda stopped and looked at Genna, the smile suddenly gone. "Genna, Mars is the best thing that ever happened to me. I mean, he's the one. He's what I've been waiting for all my life." She looked so vulnerable that Genna felt a pain radiate in her. "He's the love I thought I'd found every other time, but he's for real."

12

Genna almost cringed at the vulnerability in Belinda...and what she knew was going to happen soon. "Belinda, you're moving too fast. You need to—"

Belinda came back to Genna and cut her off. "Don't. I've heard that lecture so many times I know it by heart." She caught Genna's hand in hers and smiled at her. "Please, just this once, don't be a doctor. Don't be logical and pragmatic. Just be happy for me. I love him, Genna, really love him. Please be happy for me?"

Genna knew there was nothing she could do right now. But she'd be here after the explosion. "I want you to be happy," she said softly. "You know I do."

"And Mars makes me very happy. Someday you'll find someone who changes your world, who makes you feel as if you're finally centered and as if you've finally found what you've been looking for." Her grip tightened on Genna. "Trust me, you'll fall in love, and then you'll understand. But for now, just be happy for me. And trust me, okay?''

It wasn't Belinda she didn't trust. ''Belinda, I'm here for you, you know that.''

''Thank you,'' she said, then let Genna go when the doorbell rang. ''He's here. He's here,'' she said, and brushed at her hair. ''Do I look okay?''

''You look terrific.''

Belinda was almost bouncing up and down, she was so excited. ''Here goes,'' she whispered, then hurried over to the door.

Genna turned toward the tiny Christmas tree and stared at the ornaments as she listened to the door open, then Belinda said, ''Mars.''

Genna heard soft murmurings and closed her eyes tightly, certain she was going to be sick any minute. Then Belinda was behind her, talking again. ''Mars, I want you to meet my very best friend, sister by choice, not by birth, Genna.''

Genna steeled herself, willing herself to do this without falling apart. As she turned and opened her eyes, she saw Genna held by a man, but he wasn't Nick. He sort of looked like Nick, but he was younger and, in some way, less defined and compelling.

He smiled at Genna, but not the smile she knew. And he held out a hand to her. ''Genna, it's good to meet you...finally,'' he said in a voice that wasn't quite as deep as Nick's.

"You...you're not Nick," she found herself stammering almost incoherently.

"Nick?" Belinda said. "You know his brother? I don't understand."

"Your brother?" she whispered, and her world seemed to tip out of control.

"Nick, tall, blond, serious. Three-piece-suit type." Mars said with a crooked smile, and he didn't appear to be confused at all. "My older brother. Nicholas Marsden."

"Brother?" Genna whispered again, stunned, a feeling of hysterical relief bubbling up inside her. His brother. Nick wasn't Mars. Nick hadn't broken up with Belinda by fax. He wasn't the man she'd thought had so callously broken off the relationship.

Relief left her giddy, until she remembered her own fax and the damage she'd done with a single sheet of paper.

"I...I need to...you need to talk, and I have to—" She moved awkwardly toward Belinda's office door. She needed to get out of there and think, but as she reached the door, she turned back to Mars and Belinda. "You, Mr. Marsden—"

"Mars, call me Mars," he said with a smile that was almost as winning as his brother's smile. But not quite.

"Mars, what are your intentions toward Belinda?" The words sounded stuffy and old-fashioned, but Genna didn't care. "I need to know."

Belinda got red in the face, but Mars simply slipped his arm around her shoulders and pulled her close to his side. "I love her," he said simply.

"And?"

He narrowed his eyes on her, but he didn't back down. "I want her to marry me."

"Oh, Mars," Belinda said, turning to hug him, and Genna could tell she was crying. "Oh, I love you," she whispered on a sob.

Genna studied Mars and decided to give him the benefit of the doubt. People could change. She just hoped he'd really changed. "Don't you ever hurt her, or you'll answer to me," she said. "And it won't be by fax."

His color deepened, and she knew that he knew where his fax had gone. He hugged Belinda to him. "I won't hurt her. You've got my word on that."

"Good," she said, anxious to get out of there. "You two talk and...get things settled." She reached for the door. "I'll give you privacy."

"Genna, my brother—"

Genna cut off the man's words with a shake of her head. "You two talk," she said, then went into the office and closed the door behind her.

She stood in the middle of the messy room without a clue what to do about anything. Mars and Nick. Two different men. Two totally different people. She stared at the fax machine, wishing she'd ripped it out of the wall before she'd sent the last fax. But it was too late for that. And maybe it was too late for anything. But she couldn't just give up. Not now.

She went to the fax, grabbed a piece of blank paper and a pen, then wrote quickly.

> Disregard previous fax and everything I said. A blatant lapse of sanity on my part. I thought you were someone else, but now I understand everything. Meet me at the pier. I'll be waiting for as long as it takes...if you want to see me again.
>
> Genna.

She quickly put it in the machine and pushed in the number for Nick's office. As it started to go through the machine, she sensed someone behind her. The last thing she wanted was to face Belinda again. She couldn't even think straight, and to have to deal with unbridled happiness and joy seemed impossible for her right now.

Then a hand touched her on her shoulder, a hand she recognized without even looking at it. Then the hand reached around her and caught the fax as it came out at the front of the machine.

Maybe she was hallucinating. Then she inhaled a shaky breath and knew it wasn't an hallucination. Nick was there, right behind her, so close his heat was almost burning her back. Nick. She closed her eyes as the paper rustled. A moment later she heard him say her name.

"Genna?"

She couldn't move. Then hands were on her shoulders, gently turning her, and as she opened her eyes, she was face-to-face with Nick. A face that was etched in her memory: the strength, the blueness of his eyes, the way he had of narrowing those eyes when he was intent on something.

"You sent that fax to me?" he asked.

She could barely breathe, her chest was so tight, and her heart was hammering against her ribs. "I'm so sorry. I was wrong, really wrong."

"That's an understatement," he murmured, and she couldn't read his expression. The man had to be a killer at bluffing in business. There was no way she could tell if he was angry or indifferent or just there for information, maybe to back up his younger brother.

"Oh, Nick," she breathed, "I thought...I just assumed that you...Mars...I..." She was babbling, and suddenly he was smiling. His eyes were intense, yet his lips curved upward.

"I'm not my brother," he said. "Not even close."

She slowly lifted her hands and framed his face. The feeling of his new beard, just beginning to bristle, sent shivers through her. "No, you're not your brother," she echoed.

"The fax?"

She touched his bottom lip with her thumb and saw the unsteadiness in her own touch on him. "Ignore it. I was crazy. I was stupid. I—"

"Shhh," he said, lifting one finger to touch her lips. "Enough of that. That's the past." He exhaled. "You know, all I wanted this morning was to wake up and see you there by me. But you were gone. I hated that."

"I wanted to stay," she whispered. "But I was so stupid." She laughed, a painfully unsteady sound in her own ears. "If I was one of my patients I'd have me committed."

"Let's not go that far," he murmured. "Just tell me that everything that happened with us wasn't a lie. That it wasn't just part of you thinking you were helping your friend."

"The only lie was to myself," she whispered.

"Could you love me?" he asked suddenly.

His words hung between them, then Genna knew she had the Christmas present Belinda had wished for her. Love at first sight. Mad, passionate love at first sight. "Could you love me?"

He hesitated for a long, heart-stopping moment, then the smile came. A brilliant, shattering expression that touched her soul. "Could I? I already do. I have from the first, but I didn't realize it until it hit me over the head."

"Oh, Nick," she gasped as she moved to him,

burying her face in his chest and holding on for dear life.

He held her like that for what seemed forever, until she could ease back and look up into his face. She felt the dampness of tears on her lashes, but there was nothing but happiness in her. "Nicholas Marsden, I love you."

Without a word he drew her back to him, and when his lips found hers, she knew she'd found her home, that place in the world that was made just for her. She'd finally found it, and it was with Nick.

Christmas Eve

The party at the Marsden home was as spectacular as always. In attendance were important politicians, icons of the business community, and the Marsden family. At midnight the senior Marsdens announced their son's engagement to one Belinda Hogan, a woman in the transportation industry. And few people noticed that Nicholas Marsden left right after the announcement and that he left with a psychologist. The toasts were made, the engagement celebrated with vintage champagne.

And by the time the excitement had calmed down, Nick and Genna were where they wanted to be. They were back in the hotel suite at the Richman Towers, alone. And the only celebration they wanted was to be together.

In the shadows of the bedroom, Nick held Genna

to him, relishing the feeling of her at his side and the way he seemed to be able to inhale her essence in the air around him. Her hand rested on his bare stomach, and his leg lay heavily over her thigh.

"A very Merry Christmas," he sighed, wondering when he'd ever been happier or felt more complete.

"Yes, very merry," she echoed against his chest.

A sharp knock on the door startled him for a moment, then he remembered. He eased away from Genna, then with a quick, fierce kiss, he stood back from her and reached for the white terry cloth robe and slipped it on. "I'll be right back," he said.

He hurried through the suite to answer the door, and when he opened it, Ralph was there holding a huge, covered tray in his hands.

"Good evening, Mr. Marsden," the boy said with a wide grin. "I got everything you asked for. Just the way you wanted it."

Nick motioned Ralph into the suite. "Take everything into the bedroom, Ralph."

"Yes, sir," he said, and Nick followed Ralph into the bedroom.

Genna was sitting up in bed looking vaguely surprised, with the sheet and blanket pulled almost up to her chin. She looked at Nick with wide eyes. "What's going on?"

Ralph kept his eyes discreetly averted from Genna and crossed the room to a table and chairs positioned for a view out of the large windows. Nick went to the bed and stood by it near Genna. "It's Christmas," he said. "And I thought that we needed to start our own traditions for the season."

"Traditions?" she echoed, and he could see the color stain her cheeks.

"Yes, traditions, things we can pass on to our children and their children."

"Oh, Nick…"

"Shhhh," he said softly, brushing at her tangled hair. "Let Ralph do his thing. He owes us."

"You bet I do, sir." Ralph took the cover off the tray, then picked up something and went to the television center across from the bed. He held up a video to Nick. "Sorry, all they had was black-and-white, but if you want I can keep looking for a colored one."

Nick glanced down at Genna. "How about it? How do you like *It's a Wonderful Life,* black-and-white or colorized?"

"Oh, black-and-white. But, you—"

"That's just fine, Ralph. Put it in and start it."

"Yes, sir," he said, and in a moment the television was playing the beginning of the movie.

Ralph turned to Nick. "I got you turkey sandwiches with cranberry sauce, champagne and mistletoe. Where would you like it hung?"

Nick held out a hand. "Just give it to me. I'll take care of it."

He heard a soft chuckle from Genna, as Ralph

gave him a very anemic-looking sprig of mistletoe. "Anything else you need, sir?" the boy asked.

"I'll let you know. This is fine for now."

"Yes, sir," the boy said, then waved a hand. "And no tips necessary sir. I still owe you."

Nick nodded to him. "Thanks. Make sure the door's locked on your way out."

"Yes, sir," Ralph said, then left. Nick heard the door click shut behind the boy, then he turned to Genna.

He'd never seen anything lovelier in his life, her smiling up at him from his bed. He glanced down at the mistletoe in his hand. "Do I need this?" he asked.

She took the sprig from him, then tossed it back over her shoulder sending it somewhere into the shadows beyond the bed. "No, you don't," she said as she reached up to circle his neck with her arms and pull him down to her.

"I didn't think so," he whispered just before his lips found hers.

The passion was there immediately, no gradual building of feelings, and as it exploded in Nick, he held Genna, sensing her all around him, willing himself to get lost in the essence of the woman.

She pulled him down on top of her, the blankets gone, and skin against skin made its own heat. "Anything else you need, sir?" she said, a perfect imitation for Ralph's question moments ago.

He braced himself over her, barely aware of the television playing in the background, and looked down at her. "I've got all I need right here," he whispered. "But if I think of something later, I'll fax you."

She laughed, a marvelous sound of humor and freedom that echoed in him. "No, no more faxes," she said. "Let's do everything in person." She drew him closer, kissing him quickly, then drawing back. "I hate that newfangled technological stuff. I much prefer taking care of things one-on-one."

He laughed with her, but his humor faltered when she ran her hands over his skin and touched his stomach, then moved lower. He groaned softly, his need for her immediate and obvious. And it was her time to laugh, an unsteady sound that was muffled against the heat of his chest.

"One-on-one," she whispered. "Oh, yes."

* * * * *

COMING IN OCTOBER 1997

THREE NEW LOVE STORIES IN ONE VOLUME BY
ONE OF AMERICA'S MOST BELOVED WRITERS

DEBBIE MACOMBER

Three Brides, No Groom

Gretchen, Maddie and Carol—they were three college friends with plans to become blushing brides. But even though the caterers were booked, the bouquets bought and the bridal gowns were ready to wear...the *grooms* suddenly got cold feet. And that's when these three women decided they weren't going to get mad... they were going to get even!

"Debbie Macomber's stories sparkle
with love and laughter."
—Jayne Ann Krentz

AVAILABLE AT YOUR FAVORITE RETAIL OUTLET.

TBNG-M

MILLION DOLLAR SWEEPSTAKES
OFFICIAL RULES
NO PURCHASE NECESSARY TO ENTER

1. To enter, follow the directions published. Method of entry may vary. For eligibility, entries must be received no later than March 31, 1998. No liability is assumed for printing errors, lost, late, non-delivered or misdirected entries.

   To determine winners, the sweepstakes numbers assigned to submitted entries will be compared against a list of randomly, preselected prize winning numbers. In the event all prizes are not claimed via the return of prize winning numbers, random drawings will be held from among all other entries received to award unclaimed prizes.

2. Prize winners will be determined no later than June 30, 1998. Selection of winning numbers and random drawings are under the supervision of D. L. Blair, Inc., an independent judging organization whose decisions are final. Limit: one prize to a family or organization. No substitution will be made for any prize, except as offered. Taxes and duties on all prizes are the sole responsibility of winners. Winners will be notified by mail. Odds of winning are determined by the number of eligible entries distributed and received.

3. Sweepstakes open to residents of the U.S. (except Puerto Rico), Canada and Europe who are 18 years of age or older, except employees and immediate family members of Torstar Corp., D. L. Blair, Inc., their affiliates, subsidiaries, and all other agencies, entities, and persons connected with the use, marketing or conduct of this sweepstakes. All applicable laws and regulations apply. Sweepstakes offer void wherever prohibited by law. Any litigation within the province of Quebec respecting the conduct and awarding of a prize in this sweepstakes must be submitted to the Régie des alcools, des courses et des jeux. In order to win a prize, residents of Canada will be required to correctly answer a time-limited arithmetical skill-testing question to be administered by mail.

4. Winners of major prizes (Grand through Fourth) will be obligated to sign and return an Affidavit of Eligibility and Release of Liability within 30 days of notification. In the event of non-compliance within this time period or if a prize is returned as undeliverable, D. L. Blair, Inc. may at its sole discretion, award that prize to an alternate winner. By acceptance of their prize, winners consent to use of their names, photographs or other likeness for purposes of advertising, trade and promotion on behalf of Torstar Corp., its affiliates and subsidiaries, without further compensation unless prohibited by law. Torstar Corp. and D. L. Blair, Inc., their affiliates and subsidiaries are not responsible for errors in printing of sweepstakes and prize winning numbers. In the event a duplication of a prize winning number occurs, a random drawing will be held from among all entries received with that prize winning number to award that prize.

5. This sweepstakes is presented by Torstar Corp., its subsidiaries and affiliates in conjunction with book, merchandise and/or product offerings. The number of prizes to be awarded and their value are as follows: Grand Prize — $1,000,000 (payable at $33,333.33 a year for 30 years); First Prize — $50,000; Second Prize — $10,000; Third Prize — $5,000; 3 Fourth Prizes — $1,000 each; 10 Fifth Prizes — $250 each; 1,000 Sixth Prizes — $10 each. Values of all prizes are in U.S. currency. Prizes in each level will be presented in different creative executions, including various currencies, vehicles, merchandise and travel. Any presentation of a prize level in a currency other than U.S. currency represents an approximate equivalent to the U.S. currency prize for that level, at that time. Prize winners will have the opportunity of selecting any prize offered for that level; however, the actual non U.S. currency equivalent prize if offered and selected, shall be awarded at the exchange rate existing at 3:00 P.M. New York time on March 31, 1998. A travel prize option, if offered and selected by winner, must be completed within 12 months of selection and is subject to: traveling companion(s) completing and returning of a Release of Liability prior to travel; and hotel and flight accommodations availability. For a current list of all prize options offered within prize levels, send a self-addressed, stamped envelope (WA residents need not affix postage) to: MILLION DOLLAR SWEEPSTAKES Prize Options, P.O. Box 4456, Blair, NE 68009-4456, USA.

6. For a list of prize winners (available after July 31, 1998) send a separate, stamped, self-addressed envelope to: MILLION DOLLAR SWEEPSTAKES Winners, P.O. Box 4459, Blair, NE 68009-4459, USA.

SWP-FEB97

New York Times Bestselling Authors
JENNIFER BLAKE
JANET DAILEY
ELIZABETH GAGE

Three *New York Times* bestselling authors bring you three very sensuous, contemporary love stories—all centered around one magical night!

It is a warm, spring night and masquerading as legendary lovers, the elite of New Orleans society have come to celebrate the twenty-fifth anniversary of the Duchaise masquerade ball. But amidst the beauty, music and revelry, some of the world's most legendary lovers are in trouble....

Come midnight at this year's Duchaise ball, passion and scandal will be...

Revealed at your favorite retail outlet in July 1997.

MIRA The brightest star in women's fiction

Look us up on-line at: http://www.romance.net

MANTHOL

"For smoldering sensuality and exceptional storytelling, Elizabeth Lowell is incomparable."
—*Romantic Times*

New York Times bestselling author

LAURA CHANDLER has come home a woman—wiser and stronger than the day she left.

CARSON BLACKRIDGE is waiting—determined to win Laura back for all the right reasons.

Sweet Wind, Wild Wind

Even as Laura begins to trust in the love she has denied, the fear that history is repeating itself grows within her and she's afraid.... Afraid she'll make the same mistakes.

Available August 1997
at your favorite retail outlet.

MIRA The brightest star in women's fiction

Look us up on-line at: http://www.romance.net

SILHOUETTE... Where Passion Lives

Order these Silhouette favorites today!
Now you can receive a discount by ordering two or more titles!

SD#05988	HUSBAND: OPTIONAL by Marie Ferrarella	$3.50 U.S. ☐	/$3.99 CAN. ☐
SD#76028	MIDNIGHT BRIDE by Barbara McCauley	$3.50 U.S. ☐	/$3.99 CAN. ☐
IM#07705	A COWBOY'S HEART by Doreen Roberts	$3.99 U.S. ☐	/$4.50 CAN. ☐
IM#07613	A QUESTION OF JUSTICE by Rachel Lee	$3.50 U.S. ☐	/$3.99 CAN. ☐
SSE#24018	FOR LOVE OF HER CHILD by Tracy Sinclair	$3.99 U.S. ☐	/$4.50 CAN. ☐
SSE#24052	DADDY OF THE HOUSE by Diana Whitney	$3.99 U.S. ☐	/$4.50 CAN. ☐
SR#19133	MAIL ORDER WIFE by Phyllis Halldorson	$3.25 U.S. ☐	/$3.75 CAN. ☐
SR#19158	DADDY ON THE RUN by Carla Cassidy	$3.25 U.S. ☐	/$3.75 CAN. ☐
YT#52014	HOW MUCH IS THAT COUPLE IN THE WINDOW? by Lori Herter	$3.50 U.S. ☐	/$3.99 CAN. ☐
YT#52015	IT HAPPENED ONE WEEK by JoAnn Ross	$3.50 U.S. ☐	/$3.99 CAN. ☐

(Limited quantities available on certain titles.)

TOTAL AMOUNT	$_____
DEDUCT: 10% DISCOUNT FOR 2+ BOOKS	$_____
POSTAGE & HANDLING	$_____
($1.00 for one book, 50¢ for each additional)	
APPLICABLE TAXES*	$_____
TOTAL PAYABLE	$_____
(check or money order—please do not send cash)	

To order, complete this form and send it, along with a check or money order for the total above, payable to Silhouette Books, to: **In the U.S.:** 3010 Walden Avenue, P.O. Box 9077, Buffalo, NY 14269-9077; **In Canada:** P.O. Box 636, Fort Erie, Ontario, L2A 5X3.

Name: _____

Address: _____ City: _____

State/Prov.: _____ Zip/Postal Code: _____

*New York residents remit applicable sales taxes.
Canadian residents remit applicable GST and provincial taxes.

SBACK-SN4

Silhouette®

National Bestselling Author
JoAnn Ross

does it again with
NO REGRETS

Molly chose God, Lena searched for love and Tessa wanted fame. Three sisters, torn apart by tragedy, chose different paths...until fate and one man reunited them. But when tragedy strikes again, can the surviving sisters choose happiness...with no regrets?

Available July 1997 at your favorite retail outlet.

MJRNR

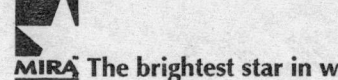

MIRA The brightest star in women's fiction

Look us up on-line at: http://www.romance.net

Coming this July...

36 HOURS

Fast paced, dramatic, compelling... and most of all, passionate!

For the residents of Grand Springs, Colorado, the storm-induced blackout was just the beginning. Suddenly the mayor was dead, a bride was missing, a baby needed a home and a handsome stranger needed his memory. And on top of everything, twelve couples were about to find each other and embark on a once-in-a-lifetime love. No wonder they said it was 36 Hours that changed *everything!*

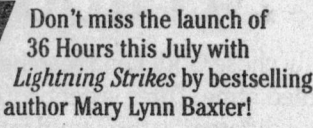

Don't miss the launch of 36 Hours this July with *Lightning Strikes* by bestselling author Mary Lynn Baxter!

Win a framed print of the entire 36 Hours artwork! See details in book.

Available at your favorite retail outlet.

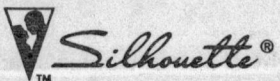

Look us up on-line at: http://www.romance.net